THE LIGHT BENDERS

Can incoming metals from outer space bring in contamination that can kill mankind? Are rockets safe from picking up invading germs? The V2 rocket has been lost in the midst of its own desolation for nearly thirty years when a piece of its metal comes into the hands of the only occupier of the bomb site. Then suddenly the metal starts to come alive, to write, to scream, to terrify the holder and the man who had come to find out why this whole deserted place had somehow gathered to itself the mark of Cain . . .

JOHN NEWTON CHANCE

THE LIGHT BENDERS

Complete and Unabridged

LINFORD
Leicester

First published in Great Britain by
Robert Hale Limited
London

First Linford Edition
published 2005
by arrangement with
Robert Hale Limited
London

British Library CIP Data

Chance, John Newton
    The light benders.—Large print ed.—
Linford mystery library
    1. Science fiction
    2. Large type books
    I. Title
    823.9′14 [F]

    ISBN 1–84395–936–4

Published by
F. A. Thorpe (Publishing)
Anstey, Leicestershire

Set by Words & Graphics Ltd.
Anstey, Leicestershire
Printed and bound in Great Britain by
T. J. International Ltd., Padstow, Cornwall
This book is printed on acid-free paper

1

I went to Nelson Street for the first time on July 19th. It was very hot and dull, the sky like copper, as if the sun shone through a fine mesh. The atmosphere was oppressive and the sounds of traffic from the highway and the river were deadened by the heat.

I left my car a quarter mile from the ruins of that curious place and walked, fanning my face with my hat. At the corner of Nelson Street I stopped and looked at the scene.

Along one side of the street reared a line of ten Victorian terrace houses, three storeys high over basement areas with rusted railings all along. Big houses, once homes of well-to-do people, when Nelson Street was the Eastern fringe of the city close to the open country. Now, beyond the end of the houses the city sprawled endlessly in the queer, reddish light, a carpet of jumbled uneven buildings with great sprouting blocks of flats and offices striding amongst the rubble below, like the Martian machines from Wells.

The other side of Nelson Street had gone, only traces of the foundations of the houses that had been here lying like forgotten bones over the big expanse cleared by German bombs first in 1917, second in 1940, and third by a V2 in 1944. Nelson Street was in a direct line with the northern loop of the river where the oil refineries and storage tanks had been. At the end of the devastated area there was a street of small terrace houses, very small by comparison with the Nelson Street Victoriana. Their windows were broken and boarded. On the east and west sides of the space, high brown brick walls reared up, the remains of some bits of houses still sticking to them, as if some giant had pulled them away too carelessly.

A few scattered wrecks of dumped cars were huddled under these walls, which guarded the yards of now deserted warehouses.

The Nelson Street area was up for

development, the whole of this scene was to be bulldozed and new glass and tin towers to go up to house high flying flat dwellers for the Council.

But for one thing. One man. Carson Grey owned the big houses in Nelson Street and lived in the middle one. The other nine were believed to be empty.

The Council should have driven him out, compulsory order pinned to the bulldozer blade, but they hesitated.

Something was wrong with Nelson Street.

That area, this July afternoon, should have been packed with the bright coloured tins of cars, and a few years back, it had been. Then gradually, they had gone. Nobody parked there any more. The tradesmen did not go to Carson Grey. The dustmen had got to staying at the end of the street while Grey drove his bins to them in his station wagon, watched them load, then took his empties back.

The children didn't play there any more. The bright weeds grew in patches, great clumps of blue and red flowers eating up the rusty wrecks of the dumped cars.

I stood there and watched Nelson Street and wondered what in hell was wrong. And what in hell was nearly right. When the moment came to walk on, down to the middle house, I felt a sudden emptiness in the stomach, the vacuum of fear.

The facts I had been given at the Town Hall offices had been strange, but too sparse to cause fear. The uneasiness I felt then was the atmosphere of Nelson Street.

I was feeling the influence that had driven back the tradesmen, driven off the cars, made the dustmen retreat to the end of the street and watch from there.

And all this had happened in the space of a few months.

I come from the Ministry of Science, but I am not a Science man. I am the man they send to find out when complaints are made of new processes causing damage or distress. Where factories suddenly start pouring bad effluent into rivers, I go there. Where farmers pour too much poison on their fields and ditches become toxic, I go there. Where radioactivity is suspected round the new stations and reactor plants, I go there. I deal with the people; the operators whose processes are causing the difficulty, and the people who are suffering. When I have all the data I can get, I go back and our chemists and science men get together and we try and find a way to ease off or stop these things going on. With new devices and chemicals, too many side effects are being produced, some highly dangerous. When this is suspected, I go and find out.

I came to Nelson Street to find out if anything was wrong.

On July 17th, a few hours before the invasion began.

★   ★   ★

I crashed on the door of the middle house with a big iron ring knocker held in a lion's mouth. When Carson Grey opened the door I thought the lion had suddenly come to life. He was big, very big, and his

5

hair was more like a mane than a sheepdog's. He peered through this ragged fringe with bright blue eyes, clear as glass marbles.

'If you're one more of those godforsaken termites from the Council, fade!' he said. 'I've nothing to say except get stuffed.'

He went to shut the door.

'I'm from the Science Ministry,' I said.

The door slammed. Then it opened again. He looked out. His light eyes bright.

'Indeed to God,' he said. 'You are?'

I gave him a card.

'Richard Wingate,' he read out, then looked at me again. 'From the Ministry! So they woke up at last, they did. Is that old crab Bedfellow still there piddling about with test tubes?'

'He retired last year.'

'In that case, come in,' he said, and turned his broad back on me.

He was in shirt sleeves and it billowed on his huge back like an underfilled barrage balloon. His hair was very dark brown and hung over his unfastened collar. He stuffed his hands into his trousers, they seemed five feet wide and narrowed down to small feet.

He opened a door to the right of the hall by raising his leg and shoving it with the sole of his shoe. Then he ambled in.

It was some room. Victorian brass lamps, fenders, irons, red plush furniture, tablecloth, pictures of Brunel, Stephenson, Faraday; gold clocks in square glass cases with spinning balances and swinging pendulums.

And everywhere in untidy piles lay books, maps, astronomical charts and a half ton of dog eared graph paper covered in heavily blotted calculations.

He picked up a slide rule and went across the room, tapping his nose with the rule, to a barrel standing in the corner. He took a brown spit mug from a shelf and smacked the tap of the barrel open with the slide rule. He watched black beer filling the mug. While it filled he stuck the rule into his open shirt and took down a second mug. He filled that then switched off the tap with the second mug and came to the table with both.

'Draught Guinness,' he said. 'Begod, there's nothin' like it as a substitute for blood.'

He was faraway, wondering, perhaps, what he was going to say to me. We drank and talked a moment about the heatwave.

'You're a science man, you say,' he said, putting his mug down. We were sitting one each side of the paper covered table. He rested his big, fat arms on a pile of books and stared at me. 'I couldn't tell them the truth. You understand that, I suppose?'

'I don't know what the truth is,' I said. 'I'm hoping to find it out.'

'I sent that crab Bedfellow my papers. A year ago. What did the bloody fool do with them?'

'He could have eaten them with his lunch sandwiches. He got very absent minded towards the end. His name,' I added quietly, 'was Bedford.'

'I suppose I sent them?' he said, staring at the window.

'I've never seen them,' I said. 'What was in them?'

He leaned further over the table towards me.

'Richardson,' he said, 'I've gone as far as I can go alone. I need help now. There isn't a lot of time left. I need some help from a man of science. You! That's why they sent you, isn't it? Then the papers must be up in your offices somewhere.'

'I've never seen any,' I said. Now this was true, but I had seen the file on Carson Grey. He had been responsible for a lot of radio astronomy developments, and had been regarded with respect by the Ministry.

But of the last couple of years my chief, Sir Francis Harcourt, had told me, 'Mad as a coot now. You probably won't get any sense out of him. Expect anything. He was always an eccentric. I don't wonder the Borough Council is worried about him, and by him.'

So I was prepared for a half-cocked genius whose brain had softened itself out. At that first interview, I seemed to have been well briefed.

At that point, having heard enough to gauge where I stood, I decided to say nothing about the Council being behind my visit. That would have lost his sympathy at once, for on the plush tablecloth there was a letter with the Town Clerk's heading. I could read the type beginning:

'As we have had no response to our previous communications regarding the development of the area containing your property, I have to advise you that unless you attend to our request within the next fourteen days we shall have no alternative but to issue a compulsory purchase order and the value of the property will then be fixed by our own Valuer.'

Across this stern note, apparently done with a brush dipped in red ink was the brief reply, 'Get stuffed.'

He must have seen me catch sight of the letter for he said, 'Oh yes. Must post that. Important business.'

Then he folded it and rummaged amongst the papers and books and maps until he found a stamped envelope, then he sealed the reply inside and threw it on the table.

'You might drop that in the box,' he

said. 'I didn't think they'd have the sense to send anyone. You a radio man, Richards?'

'No. But you'd hardly expect them to send a top radio man. You'd both be fighting all the time.'

He roared with laughter all of a sudden. It split his face in half and he looked as if he had sixty teeth at least.

I have not said yet that I noticed anything strange in that place because I wasn't sure my feelings were not the reaction of my own prickly fears. Apart from the atmosphere of Nelson Street, which could be imaginary, dealing with Carson Grey was like juggling a grenade with the pin out.

One had only to put a foot wrong, and the explosion would blow the inquisitor out of the front door.

I would admit now that throughout my association with Grey, I was tensed, almost frightened of him. An offer to help him when I knew little professionally on the subject was dangerous, it looked then.

It *was* dangerous, I know now, but not because of him.

'I'm just an all round stooge,' I said, when he'd roared himself out.

'You know this business about Sirius?' he said, leaning across the table again. 'Signals. Got a suspicion they've been trying to get in touch for years.'

'I thought Sirius was a dead star.'

'The only way to tell if anything is dead is kick it,' he said. 'My probe lines intersect there. My angles are acute as a needle. I use a vernier scale magnified millions of times by six computer banks. I don't think they're wrong, but you can't be sure with bloody machinery. It only wants one missed kick to put the damn thing out eighty million miles. You realize that?'

'I know the possibility. Nothing's perfect.'

He started off on a lot of figures and trigonometry, differentials and spectrum analysis. That sort of stuff gets past me like a fast ball. That was not what I had come to find out.

'Could be from beyond, if the intersection carries on a few million more,' he said. 'Or could be a reflection. Its impossible to be quite sure. Using laser quite a bit, too. Good probe, but they're all crude when one considers what they're trying to find out. Needles in haystacks and turning the straws with a dinner fork. Almost as bad as looking for Truth.'

He got up and started walking about the room, missing the big, padded furniture like a ship dodging rocks.

'I'm rich,' he said. 'My mother was a brewer's daughter I couldn't do this otherwise. Nobody pays for ideas now.'

He stopped near me and glared down.

'You're not from the Council are you?'

'No. I'm the Ministry. You saw the card.'

He stayed there glaring, then eased and moved away.

'We can't have them here now,' he said. 'These next few days are vital. Our position is critical. We shan't occupy it again for another thirty five years. And there's this hairy band of bulldozing twits thinking of a piddling little bit of ground like this! It makes one weep to think of it.'

For a moment I thought he really did

weep. I don't think I would have been surprised.

'They won't come yet,' I said. 'Not while I'm here. They won't go against the Ministry.'

It was a mislead, for I was operating from the Council Offices, but I was right in saying the Council wouldn't do any more till I gave the word. The idea of giving the wrong word crossed my mind and I quaked a little inside at the thought of the wild Irish rage that would then burst forth on me.

'You sure of that?' he said.

'Quite.'

He crossed the room to a glass fronted and curtained tallboy that the Victorians had kept their sheet music in. When he opened the door I saw the inside was lined with a thick layer of white glasswool board, like compressed snow.

He lifted out a thin bent piece of metal and put it on the plush table cloth. It seemed to have been burnt blue on the outer curved side, and the inside was yellow with a piece of curved channel metal riveted to the main piece. It appeared to have been torn out of a much larger piece.

'Dural,' he said. 'It's a bit of a V2 that fell here on August 15th, 1944. Lift it up.'

It weighed very light, but there was something odd about the feel of it, as if some faint electric current ran in it. It sent a tingle up my fingers and sinews to the elbow.

'Listen to it!' he said tensely. 'Hold it to your ear.'

I did. The thing was humming, a kind of ringing hum. It was the vibration of this that had made my fingers tingle.

'Hell!' I said. 'What's the matter with it?'

He swung a chair round with one hand and straddled it, leaning his fat arms on the back. His head stuck forward more like the lion doorknocker than ever.

'Its contaminated,' he said. 'In that flight of August 15th it picked up something out there.'

He pointed to the sky through the window.

'That's a long time ago,' I said.

'It takes time for maggots to develop,' he said.

I took another close look at the piece of burnt and twisted metal. Apart from the yellowish surface on the inside, which was a manufactured finish, I saw nothing on it.

'You won't see anything,' he said. 'But they're there. They've got into the atomic structure of the metal. That's why it hums. You can feel its getting hot, too.'

I hadn't noticed it, for the day itself was so hot and oppressive, but I held it against my cheek and found he was right.

'Isn't this dangerous?' I said, putting the metal down. 'If it goes on getting hotter there will be combustion sooner or later.'

'Its taken nearly thirty years to get that warm,' he said. 'You needn't worry yet. The temperature is being raised by the changing of the structure within.'

'What's changing it?'

'Its contaminated,' he said again. 'It caught a bug out in space and its germinated over the years.'

I picked the metal up and listened

16

again. It was like a single, steady note of the old raid sirens. An association of ideas, perhaps, but the likeness was certainly there.

He reached out suddenly and took it from me. He took the piece between his big hands and bent it, first one way, then the other as if trying to weaken it so that it would break. After several bends he handed it back.

'Listen to the note,' he said.

I did. It was much higher now.

'Heat from the bending,' he said, and got up. 'All very interesting.' He took the metal and put it back in the cabinet. He shut the door carefully, I noticed.

'Phenomenon number one,' he said. 'I have others. And that out there — ' he pointed through the window to the ragged blazing weeds of the devastated area, ' — that is phenomenon number x. They talk of compulsory purchase. They wouldn't if they knew the truth. They'd run miles.' He turned away suddenly, and smacked his pockets. 'Where the hell did I put that?'

He walked out. I was alone in the

room, all sound deadened by its deep richness. It was hard to think of this room as being in the middle of a busy, screaming city.

I looked out of the windows at the ragged grandeur of the waste ground. It looked as normal as a bombsite can look that has run to seed and wilderness in the middle of dying buildings. There was, at least, nothing abnormal to be seen there.

Maggy came in then. I was surprised to see a girl there, and surprised too at the girl herself. She had long gold hair which hung and hid half her face. One thick eyebrow showed over an eye smoky black painted with a blue lid. She smiled lopsidedly, for she had daubed her mouth on out of the level, but for all that mishandling it was a look that shook me. She was tall and plump with big breasts and belly and pushed all three at me in unmistakable welcome. She wore a white linen dress with small buttons running all up the front. The top foot of it, almost, was not done up and she appeared to have nothing on underneath.

'Hallo,' Maggy said. 'Who are you?'

She put her hand up and lifted the hair away so she could look at me with both eyes. They were very dark blue, and even with the heavy painting, would make any man look again. The mispainted mouth, big and loose had a nude sexual appeal which the lopsidedness seemed to emphasize.

'Richard Wingate,' I said.

She pointed at the open door. The hair fell again.

'That's my father,' she said, and came nearer. 'Are you married?'

'No.'

'Neither is he,' she said. 'My mother comes sometimes. What do you do?'

'I'm at the Science Ministry.'

She wasn't interested in that, but stood there watching me intensely. She put her hands on her thighs and the undone dress opened so that I could see the shining valley between the hills of her breasts.

'Do you live here?' I said.

'I help my father. He's not really very good at maths. I am.'

That was surprising. She was surprising. I was to learn that most things she

19

did were surprising, and done in surprising ways.

'He's in contact with aliens,' she said. 'Did he tell you?'

'No. What aliens?'

'He thinks they're on Sirius, but you can't be sure at that distance.' She stood dead in front of me as I stood by the window, then lifted her hair aside. 'Kiss me,' she said. 'Come on. I like it.'

For a moment I just stood there. She got hold of my face in her hands and did the kissing, plastering her lips over mine in a writhing sensual joy until I responded. She worked her body against me with an almost savage sensuality.

Then she broke, pushed me in the chest and smacked me across the face so that it stung.

'Sex beast,' she said, and turned away.

It needed a more agile and adaptable mind than mine to work that out, to think of an answer, or even of anything to say at all. With the heat of the kiss still running in me like a hot wave, it was hard even to think.

'He's been in touch for a long time,'

she said, turning back as if nothing had happened in between the mention of Sirius and now. 'He's made a translating machine. It works on the principle that thoughts make words, so he goes back to the thoughts and it seems they don't have words so that there's the common base. But with aliens it doesn't quite work. He abandoned it.'

'Do you mean he's been getting signals?'

'He's been getting signals, but I don't believe they're coming from outside.' She sounded and looked petulant.

'Any reason?'

'He doesn't believe. He pretends.'

'Did he tell you that?'

'No. He keeps on pretending.'

'Where are the signals coming from?'

She watched me.

'There's a man I hate. He comes here, checks figures. There are a lot of figures. A hell of a lot.' She stood there smoothing her thighs with her hands, still watching me.

'Yes, but where are the signals coming from?'

'Here.'

'Alien signals?'

'Yes.'

'You mean the contamination of the rocket?'

'Its more than that, you fool. Father keeps kidding himself its from way out, because even he's getting afraid to acknowledge the truth.'

'What exactly do *you* know about this?'

She smiled.

'I know what they think. I can know what you think, too. The machine. It translates thinks. Human thinks. Father didn't think of that side-effect. He's concentrating too much on the signals.'

'Was the translator making anything at all of the alien signals?'

'Not in so many words. Not in so many thinks. But there is a similarity with certain human signals that are sent out secretly at certain times.'

'What times?'

'When you're getting things ready for an invasion. Like that.'

From her behaviour I would have been justified in thinking of her as a nut case, but there was an intensity about what she said, and what she did.

'Just a minute. How can there be an invasion if the invaders are here already?'

'That's for you to work out, darling. Not me. I'm just a simple girl with a passion for passion.'

'Don't be facetious, please. Obviously you know a good deal about this. I'm very anxious to know, too.'

'Is that what you came for?'

'I came from the Ministry to contact your father. If what you say is true in any degree, then this is very much my business. You see, we have departments which have been waiting — no, I should say working on such possibilities.'

'You expect trouble?'

'That's much too definite. I'm talking about a Possibility Dept. We've been trying to get signals from other worlds for many years. We have to consider the possibility that the signals have been received but not answered.

'Stars die, perhaps with people still on them. Our signals give signs of a vigorous life here. The watchers can see we have a long way to go before Earth cools off. So the possibility is that the watchers get the idea our Earth will suit them better than their dying one. Best to get off the sinking ship if there's another handy.'

'And you mean they'll be hostile, like Men?'

'That's the possibility, isn't it?'

'So you've got a department trying to work out how they might do it?'

'They dabble with ideas all the time. Facts, analyses are given to them. They use their imaginations.'

'And you?'

'No. I'm just the wandering boy. Department to Department. Anybody uses me.'

I sat down in the chair Grey had used. She looked down at me.

'I don't really know anything, but that it's coming. Father might know, but he's a coward. He won't think of it. That's why I can't get the machine to tell. His thinks somersault, turn over backwards so as not to see the truth.'

'But he talked about it openly. The contamination. He showed me the metal.'

'Yes. But he won't go any farther. He still pretends it's way out in space. A long way off, so that he's got plenty of time.'

'But he said only a few days!'

'That's more than it will be.'

She lifted the brief skirt, swung a leg across mine and then sat on my lap, straddling. She grabbed my face again and started to smear her lipstick on my mouth.

'For God's sake!' I said, holding her back a bit.

'Have me,' she said urgently. 'Then he won't try any more. He's always trying. If there was you, he wouldn't have the nerve to keep on.'

Her breasts almost burst out of the open dress as I held her arms beside her.

'Who? What man?'

'The man I hate. He always tries to get me.'

'You can fend him off, for heaven's sake.'

'It's difficult with him. You see, I had him once. He was my tutor at college. I hated him. I hated him so much I wanted to have him and both be found out. So I did, in his rooms, and the Principal walked in. So he got the sack and I was sent down. My father was mad. But that fool kept coming round because he couldn't understand I'd done it for kicks. He thought I must have been in love with him, the stupid idiot. I kept telling him, but he thinks it's my fun. My fun! Can you imagine that?'

'I can imagine almost anything,' I said. 'Get up.'

She pressed hard and my grip on her arms gave. She grabbed me tight, wrestling me against the chair back.

'You want me, don't you? Well, do it for me! I can't stand him! You don't know how — '

She went on huskily urgent, and then past her golden hair I saw Carson Grey come into the room.

'Leave the man alone, Maggy,' he said, showering a sheaf of papers on the table. 'There'll be time for that later.'

She broke, sat back on me, lifted her hair and looked at me. Then she smiled, almost laughed, got up and went out.

'Impetuous. Impulsive,' said Grey,

sorting the papers. 'I should have called her Diana the Huntress. Now take a look at these calculations.'

I wiped lipstick off my face with my handkerchief. She had smeared it on like paint.

'She said there would be an invasion, according to signals you've received or intercepted.'

'Yes. I play it down for her. Don't want her to be frightened and buzz off. I need her here. There's nobody else that would do, you see. Now you've come, we shall have enough.'

'Enough to deal with an invasion?' I said, incredulous.

He stroked his chest thoughtfully and stared out of the window.

'That we can't tell yet,' he said. 'We don't know half enough. But we shall find it out in the next couple of days. It won't be pleasant finding, but it's got to be done.'

'Look, if you're really serious, I can get you all the help you want, Grey.'

'You can't,' he said. 'We've no phone.'

'I can go back to the office — '

'Not now,' he said. 'We can't let you out any more. You're here. You stay. If you try to go I'll blow your bloody head off.'

And from the mess of papers and maps, books and rubbish he took up a small automatic pistol and pointed it straight at my eyes.

2

It was the final eccentricity, or lunacy. I just looked at the gun and his grinning face and something crawled up the back of my neck. Then he laughed and put the gun down.

'She has what she wants,' he said. 'I have to make that agreement with her or she could put a spanner in all my works. We can't afford that now, none of us. She wants you. You stay. Be sensible. Don't try anything because I hate being forced into anything. Have a cigarette.'

I took one from his crushed packet.

'I'm not mad,' he said, as if reading my thinking exactly, 'but this work produces strange tensions. Bound to. Its not natural work, as we understand nature. This is a different kind of nature. A new one on us.'

'What sort of one?'

'Nebulous. Nothing firm. I've applied usual natural laws but they don't seem to work. They won't identify. All the natural results we can get are the sound and the increasing heat. That could identify anything.'

'You also made the point that whatever it is has been incubating getting on for thirty years.'

'That needn't apply. Freezing can keep the thing thirty years. If it was frozen when it came in it's been buried in the ground for years. That could maintain its original temperature a long time. No real problem there.

'The real problem is, what is it?'

'Can you identify the sound?'

'Not identify. It's like the sound you get when tracking stars by radio. Sort of outer fringe echo. I don't know what causes that. Some kind of frequency beat. There's a hell of a lot of noises out there.'

'Your daughter says you have made some sense of signals you've been picking up.'

'True. But they weren't intended for us, I'm guessing. We have intercepted signals being sent between units of, say, an army. That's what I'm thinking. That's what my think machine said, but that robot was too interested in human thought.'

'You could have intercepted some kind of war signals,' I said, 'but what gave you the idea they might be directed against us? There are millions of stars.'

'The carrier waves on these signals aren't normal radio mush,' he said. 'They're a sound, like on that metal, like the red drift echoes. Like that.'

He got up and went to the window.

'I mean,' he went on, 'it's one hell of a coincidence that this alien sound is way out on the fringe of things, and yet is also out there.'

He pointed to the weed-grown lot. The sky was thick, smoky copper red, as if something was coming down on it from above.

I got a sudden alarm about the whole thing, an inexplicable fear of something imminent. My coward's mind twisted around to try and prove I had nothing to be frightened of.

'If these signals are coming from so far out,' I said, 'then any invaders couldn't reach here for a million years. Have you thought of that?'

'They have been travelling near thirty years,' he said. 'You keep forgetting that. Also an advance guard must have been standing off this poor old orb when the V2 came in here.'

'You mean this attack has been planned over centuries?'

'It seems like it.'

'Funny no one else seems to have any track of it.'

'No one else has my equipment,' he said, and tapped his head. 'It starts here. That's where the difference is. Modern development follows the beaten path and then beats it further. I wander off, find another way that might be shorter. This time I struck lucky.'

'If this thing is a threat, why haven't you said anything?'

'Because, dear fellow, who would take any notice of a half sozzled eccentric Irishman? Can you imagine the bureaux clattering in a dance of agitation, preparing defences against God knows what? They wouldn't do a thing. They might have me examined. I'm one bloody great bag of sheer astonishment that they even got as far as sending you.'

'That was because the Council thought — '

'The Council?' he shouted. 'So they do come into it, the screaming noddies! So they — '

'They thought there was contamination out on the plot over there!' I shouted him down.

He stopped in surprise.

'All right, all right,' he said, surprised at getting his own back in his face. 'What contamination?'

'It was the way the tradesmen drifted off, the cars didn't park any more, the dustmen wouldn't come. All these things began to look funny.'

'It was that, was it?' he said, startled. 'Hell! They said it was because it wasn't worth coming just for one house and two people in it.'

'I suppose they couldn't really think of anything else to say. Most people would think of an excuse not to go into a haunted house, but they wouldn't say they were frightened of anything like a ghost.'

'A ghost.' He frowned and ruffled his untidy hair. 'Quite a simile, eh? Quite a likeness. Something you might hear and feel the temperature of, but can't touch. I hadn't thought of that. Hadn't thought of that at all.'

He started to march about the room, muttering things about ghosts, spirits, light rays, human senses.

'Don't let it divert you,' I said. 'This is no ghost, from what I gather. I can't see a phantom scaring off a hundred different car owners, all scrambling for somewhere to park.'

'No, no,' he said. 'The simile is scientific, concerning the haunted not the haunting. A matter of sensitiveness to frequencies. Now that fool Potson said the place smells of ghosts. He said he'd seen ghosts, but that was a little while back. I didn't connect it.'

'Who's Potson?'

'He was Maggy's tutor,' he said, and laughed. 'She got him blown. He helps here when I want checkings. He'd come anyway if she put a finger up. He'd beg, too, and bark, I shouldn't wonder. But it keeps him coming, that's the thing, and he knows his numbers.'

He ambled around the room, staring at the floor and talking. He was a worried man, but not personally worried. He was worried because he couldn't understand what he was finding out.

And because he felt he wouldn't have time to find out.

'In the evening, when the traffic's quiet, I'll take you out there. We'll stand a while. You'll see then what I mean. Potson sweated so he fell on his knees. It was pathetic, but he wasn't used to it. You might, too. We'll see.'

He walked to the door.

'Come. I'll show you round.'

He led the way up the long staircase that doubled on itself four times and reached the top floor. He opened a door on the left and went in.

It was dark in there, except for a number of dull white illuminated circles like table tops. There were six, and they stretched into an incredible distance.

'We knocked the walls down,' he said. 'These are our scanners.'

In the middle of each table there was a tilted bowl made of a fine wire network. It was like a radio telescope on a minute scale. They turned slowly, not together, but each at a different angle.

When I got used to the weird light, I saw that the table tops were themselves white bowls, and that the light was actually being sent out from the base of the tiny scanners and reflected from the pure white bowls of the tables.

'We get an immense magnification by that laser adaptation transmitting from the receiver bowl here — ' he pointed to the scanner. 'Which gives two pictures one small — here — '

At this point he flicked switches out of my sight in the darkness, but somewhere beneath the nearest scanner. The whole wall to the left of us suddenly leapt into startling colour.

It was not like a reproduction, but as if the whole side of the house had been cut away and the house itself was drifting in the dark blue nothing of space, with stars golden, red, blue, green — indescribable tints — drifting towards us and passing us at each side.

It made me feel suddenly dizzy and sick.

'Our beams are searching, you see,' he said, 'which gives the impression that we are moving forward amongst the stars. Fascinating. Rather like starlight reflections on the dimpled water passing our boat.'

I hadn't time for this bogus poetry. The atmosphere of that place was tense. It was also a damned sight hotter than the rest of the day, which was close enough.

'Take your jacket off,' he said, seeing me wipe my face with my handkerchief. 'You won't need it.' He laughed again.

'What are we watching?' I took my coat off and draped it over my arm. I also loosened my collar and tie.

'Sirius and surrounds,' he said. 'It's coming up quite big in the middle, you see.'

A central star was focussed so that it seemed to stand out in three dimensions from the rest of the depthless void. It came like a ball of golden fire hanging in nothing, so that I felt it was possible to reach out and take it out of that staggering scene of vastness.

But it came no larger, as if we had stopped moving forward. There was just the sound of the mini-motors driving the scanners and nothing else.

'Now look,' he said. 'Observe the central star very closely. You can just see the shadow of another star a few million miles behind it. You see?'

'Like the edge of the sun in eclipse,' I said. 'The Dog Star doesn't quite cover it.'

'Now we'll get a magnification of that side where the edge shows,' he said, snicking switches. 'This is bad detail. Fuzz. But you can't blow it up and keep the detail.'

Above the weird wall scene, slanting down towards us was a big cathode ray tube. The picture came up in colour, but if I hadn't already seen the whole in the big picture I couldn't have made head or tail of this one.

It was like a sliver of a new moon seen

through dense cloud, and from it curved out a streamer of golden gas or some such element. Everything glittered with the gold which gave the impression that the gas streamer was moving slowly towards us.

'You get the drift?' he said, and laughed shortly.

'What is it — gas?'

'If I knew, we need no longer be in doubt. We can only spot it there because of the concentration. As it travels out in space it spreads and thins and finally we can't see it. But its coming, visible or not.'

'Coming this way?'

'It's the direction, so far as we can check. And to link up, there's the trace downstairs, and outside. Its a hell of a coincidence, isn't it?'

'Do your computers confirm this?'

'They do. But you can't trust damned machines. They must be checked in a thing like this. I haven't room to get any more computer checkers in so I use the human machine. Anyway, its a double check to have two different types of machinery.'

'And your human calculators confirm, too?'

'Within limits. Neither of them can get an exact reading over the distance, because what we're measuring is small, and thins right out into isolated elements as it enters deeper space.'

'But what is it?'

'I've tried a spectrum analysis by using laser, and there seems to me a metal element and there's a hydrogen trace. There again, you can't be sure. It could be a like element.'

'If there's metal do you mean that indicates a manufactured article in that stream?'

He laughed, but it was like a sneer.

'Suppose that stream is made up of manufactured articles,' he said. 'Now is the time to shake!'

'You're crazy,' I said. 'That would be a fantastic armada!'

'It would indeed, my friend. And I am convinced that that is exactly what it is, and that the radiation out in that plot is guiding it here!'

'Any proof?'

'We have made a good many calculations. Computers and men agree to within twenty four hours, which is near enough. I'm thinking either tonight or tomorow night we shall know for sure. So be patient.'

He smiled and his mouthful of teeth gleamed in the backlight from the scanner basins.

'You're almost looking forward to it,' I said, wiping my face again. I don't know whether it was the heat, the weird layout of the scene, or plain fear that made me sweat. Perhaps all three.

'Not looking forward,' he said, stopping his vast grin. 'No. But anything's better than waiting.'

He went to the door.

'I'll show you Potson,' he said. 'And the computers. You won't like either.'

*   *   *

The first time I saw Potson I thought he was a woman. I had thought of Grey as fat, but Potson was fatter. Fat, rounded like a woman, wearing nothing but trousers and his smooth skin shining from oil, the mistake was understandable.

He sat in a chair under a lamp, wearing dark glasses. His fair, almost albino hair overhung the black lenses as he stared at me. Maggy was rubbing his shoulders with some sort of oil. She watched me and smiled.

Grey introduced us.

'From the Ministry? Oh, splendid,' Potson said and grinned as he held his hand out.

Maggy reached round and rubbed his belly with oil so he had to lean back. So we didn't shake hands. He shrugged.

'We've found there is danger of getting burns from some of the equipment, sort of sunburn,' he said. 'That's what it feels like though it doesn't actually burn.'

'It just makes you fat,' Grey said, staring at him.

'Does it?' I said, surprised.

'Yes. It'll be interesting to know why. It's always interesting to know why.'

'It doesn't make me fat,' Maggy said. 'I'm always like this.' She laughed and pushed her tummy out to make herself look fat. Then she went on oiling him.

He was watching me from behind the dark glasses.

'Do they know at the Ministry?' he said.

'No. This is news.'

'You're done,' she said, and turned away to a lavatory basin on the wall.

He stood up. He was about five eleven and from his almost cherubic face looked around thirty-five.

'Let's get down,' Grey said, turning his back.

'Down to the torture dungeons,' Potson said, coming behind Maggy to the door.

She came beside me and we all went down the stairs into the hallway again. Grey's study where I had been lay on the left at the bottom. On the right of the stairs the kitchen passage ran to the back of the house. On the right was another door.

Grey opened this.

'Watch your step,' he said, and just stood there on the threshold.

It was in fact the only place to stand. The floor had been ripped up as if a bomb had been through it, leaving edges of broken joists and laths just inside the door and along the front wall.

The scene was immense. The hole in the floor was continuous for the next four houses. Wall after wall had been hacked through, leaving huge arches of ripped brickwork, here and there propped with timber struts, as if somebody had been in a hurry to stop the upper floors falling in and had forgotten the affair later. In this great long hall formed from the ground floors and the basements a vast computer room had been built. Down on the basement floors there were ranges of machines, tapes, cameras, projectors, computers, accounting machines and tables where apparently the human mathematicians worked.

The air was tense with the hum of electrical activity, but the heat was intense. It seemed to enfold me like an invisible blanket. I felt I wanted to throw off all my clothes and just stand there in it.

'Ladder down,' Grey said, pointing to his feet.

He started to go down a high pair of steps leaning up against the broken threshold. The girl went next, I followed and Potson came last. On the floor below the heat was even thicker. I use that word because it felt like that more than it did a burn from a fire, or just excessive heat such as in a furnace room.

Grey started to walk along the ranks of the machines, saying what part each one took in his whole makeup of the space searcher.

Machines I had seen before. I saw them every day somewhere or other, even if not hooked up like this. But what fascinated me was to stand and look up at the long series of decorated plaster ceilings running away in either direction, divided only by the remnants of the hanging brick walls. The windows above us seemed to have been blocked up so that no one from the street might see into this hall of figures.

Potson had a couple of working desks, set together in an L with a swivel chair commanding the situation. The desks were covered in papers, tables, references, slide rules and a scattered mass of lurid paperbacks. He picked one up.

'Relaxing,' he said, and threw it down. 'One can get too close to figures.'

I noticed none of them appeared to be science fiction. Perhaps he was frightened of that subject.

As he walked Grey undid his shirt right down, pulled it out of his trousers and flapped the front. The heat was growing in me, too. The machines hummed noisily though there was no direct source of the sound. It seemed to be trembling in the atmosphere, like the heat.

Grey pointed to slow rolling tapes and explained what they did. The floor was gritty with plaster and mortar dust which must have been continually falling from the roughly broken out brickwork above.

We came back to Potson's desk.

'Sit down,' Grey said.

I sat in the swivel chair. Potson shovelled a lot of papers across to me. Maggy sat on one of the desks and watched. Grey stood opposite across the desk, picked up a slide rule and began pointing to figures on the papers. They were so immense as to be meaningless to me. The mathematical hieroglyphics were even worse.

'Put it in words of one syllable and cut out the brackets,' I said.

Potson took over from Grey, standing sideways, pointing with a ballpoint. His explanation was lucid and simple.

'If you plot a curve based on these figures you will see that the drift which has been observed beyond Sirius is coming this way,' he said. 'At the outset, fifty years back, we have calculated, the original stream started out and no real direction was discernible for many years.'

'A pilot stream,' Grey said. 'The mainstream followed later. You have to remember that what we see on the screens upstairs happened several years ago.'

'Forty-nine years plus,' Potson said.

'So that if these are men in space ships, and they started, say at age twenty-five, they'll be seventy-five now,' I said. 'Not a very fearsome project, facing a horde of old men.'

'It could be that they don't age at the

same rate,' Grey said.

'There's no reason why they have to be men,' Maggy said. 'Man is a mutation, a mistake. He should have been on four legs but something went wrong somewhere. It doesn't follow this mutation happened on other planets.'

'Obviously,' I agreed. 'Also they could have passed through this mutation stage and really achieved a worthwhile being. In which case, as you say, we should be up against something quite formidable.'

Grey laughed suddenly.

'You talk as if they won't arrive for another fifty years!' he said. 'But by God, they're waiting outside now! Right out there!'

He pointed up to the line of shuttered windows.

'If you follow the checking stages,' Potson said, 'you will see that the mainstream must be within a few thousand miles of us now. As we calculate they have travelled many millions of miles in only fifty years, a few thousand could be covered in a second or less.'

'We are only one of a galaxy of millions

of stars,' I said. 'Why should it come to us? What sorted us out?'

'That old damned rocket,' Grey said. 'It could be that out of the millions of stars only one sent up a tin porpoise high enough for somebody far off to notice it. Or more likely the rocket was contaminated by accident, a drift from far off that came in too close.

'But this contamination has been signalling back. No doubt of that now.'

'One point,' I said. 'Your figures establish this expedition set out forty-nine years back. Right. But the rocket wasn't fired till nineteen years later.'

'A probe stream perhaps,' Grey said. 'One which left this contamination trace which the rocket picked up. The rocket came down, the trace incubated and signalled back. So the drifting stream signalled back to the other streams that were heading for our constellation.

''Avast ye airy lubbers!' it flashed, 'there's a living world down here. One such as we have been looking for. Come on in. The water's fine!''

He turned and stared at the slow

rolling tapes in a computer cabinet.

'Father puts it so that a child can understand,' Maggy said, and laughed. 'But that group there is the one. There!'

She pointed with a blood red nail to the final equation on the last sheet, and pushed aside those almost covering it.

'The computers agree with it,' she went on. 'It gives us twenty-four hours before the come-in starts.'

'And if it's out there now, as you say,' I protested 'why can't we see it? Where is the radio astronomy, the space radar, the stand-off detectors? They've given no signals of something there. Your radar detects it fifty light years off but not near us now.'

'There's an old saying about not seeing the wood for the trees,' said Grey. 'Or you can blow up an atomic structure so big that you can only see the spaces in between the items. It's one of these two. We shan't know which until it's here!'

Potson's fat, shiny belly was going in and out as if he had been running. Perhaps it was fear that made him breathe so hard. He put his fat arm round

Maggy's waist and she put her hand on his as it lay there, as if to keep it there. She smiled at me.

What the hell that meant I couldn't tell. If she hated the man so much how did she let him make these affectionate gestures? It was a puzzle. It was a pleasant shift of the mind from a vast and terrifying problem to a small, sweaty human one.

But even that one I couldn't explain.

'So what do we do?' I said.

'What can we do?' said Grey, and laughed in my face. 'Nobody's going to believe me. Me of all people. The old original drunken looney from Dublin, bursting into tears at The Kerry Dances.'

'You might have been treated better if you hadn't spent so much energy telling big bureaux to get stuffed and pull their fingers out and all the rest of the contemptuous crap!' I shouted at him. 'If they think you're a drunken dolt now it's because you told them you were! Don't blame them if they thought you'd proved it, too!'

The girl burst into a fit of laughter.

Grey glared and then laughed too, but it was a hard laugh, and it stopped very short as he wiped his hot face.

'I'll screw your bloody head off one day,' he said, turning away. 'You're all the same. A touch of the bureaucratic brush and your arses are glued in the groove. I'm sick of the lot of you. Sit down, gum bottom. Stick in your ruddy seat and let it all happen. Let's all sit on our bums and wait. After all, what good can we do? Leave it all in the In tray and we'll all sit in the Out. Bring on the tea! You have nothing to lose but your brains!' He leant against a brick pier. 'It'll be either tonight or tomorrow. Between eleven and three a.m. That's the time we face the stream.'

'Now you've let the steam blow, listen,' I said. 'I'll go back to my office and check if any of this contamination has been traced on other space material that's come back. It's important to do that, you must agree.'

The girl shoved Potson away so that he fell against the far desk. Then she came to me.

'Oh, but you mustn't go,' she said, with

an odd smile. 'You'd never come back.'

'I'll give you my word,' I said, turning back to Grey. 'That check is important. There's another thing. There may be corroborative evidence in our departments which hasn't been understood. What you've found could be the key they're waiting for.

'And third: if this discovery is corroborated, the whole resources of the Ministry could be put behind you.'

'You mean they'd move in the tea machine?' Grey said, showing all his teeth again. 'Hail Columbia! bird thou never wert in triplicate. Most impressive. What makes you think I care if your lot corroborate anything? At the most we've got thirty hours. They couldn't do anything in that time.'

'And what exactly do you propose to do?' I said. 'You're stuck here, three of you — '

'Four, darling,' the girl said and laughed.

'You're all cracked as a crazy path!' I said. 'What can you do?'

'You don't seem to get the drift,'

Potson said, earnestly. 'We haven't got anything that would convince an official. We have a sound, a feel of heat, some figures and movement on a screen from fifty years ago. We have put a construction on these frailties. Your official must think first that we could be entirely wrong. Heat and sound are generated by odd natural occurrences. It doesn't have to be alien.'

True. When he said that I realized that I had been swayed, mesmerized by the imagination and emotional approach of Grey and his daughter. The proofs were thin indeed. So I saw it then when Potson spoke.

'To put it as Euclid,' said Maggy, 'we have no proof until the Things come.'

'She thinks they'll be hordes of huge handsome men,' said Grey, mockingly.

Potson peered at me through the dark glasses.

'What do you really think?' he said anxiously.

'I've been sold an idea,' I said. 'I think it ought to be gone into thoroughly.'

'Not by those goons,' Grey said sourly.

'Not at any price. I've served my time with the stinkers. They'll not have another chance to block me. There's a letter upstairs now threatening to bulldoze me out of here. That could have happened by now. What then?' He flung a hand towards his lines of equipment.

'It hasn't happened,' I said, losing my temper. 'That's why I'm here — '

'So you *are* a Council goon!' he bawled. 'I thought so all along.'

Then he reeled off into a blasting denunciation of all Councils and bureaucrats. It was a furious, mad delivery. It shook me back. This was not satirical commentary now but a searing shower of hate.

When he stopped I let it simmer a minute.

'Suppose you're dead right about all this invasion,' I said. 'You're not going to let hatred for all Civil Servants get in the way of warning ordinary people, are you?'

'There are no ordinary people,' Grey said. 'Just sheep. Talking sheep. If the earth was flat and these sheep heard about my invasion, they'd all run the same way — off the edge. The civil servants would stay behind, perhaps, to read out a few byelaws in triplicate.' He banged the piece of broken wall with his fist. He was thinking of something else from what he talked about. His was a multiway mind.

In that hot, electric atmosphere, one could think almost anything, as if the fingers of the atmosphere got into the mind and irritated certain nerves and lines, like the muscles in a dissected frog's leg.

The girl and Potson were watching me, she with an almost odd look of relish, and he as if waiting for some answer of dramatic importance.

In that atmosphere, madness seemed sane. I had been trapped by intention, but here as I looked at the three of them I had the sudden feeling that if I tried to get out they would fall on me and tear me apart.

How the hell sane people could get such ideas as that I can only blame on that weird air in the place. I've never thought such things before, and realizing it I wondered if I had been influenced into being as crazy as they were.

'You'll find it very difficult to withstand the pressures this thing creates in the mind,' Grey said, as if he saw my thoughts written on my face. 'It's near madness, if you're clever enough to define the limits of that state. I always think mind states are infinity signs, meaning anything . . . The time is six forty. Did you expect it to be so late?'

It shocked me. I would have said an hour had passed, perhaps a little more, but three and a half seemed impossible.

'Time is meaningless in this house now,' he said. 'The aura accelerates the mind so much it becomes nightmare quick and time relativity begins to fade. The only thing to keep in mind is that outside this house, there is real time, and very little of it left.'

'If you think that, why sit here doing nothing?' I said. 'Get in touch with the authorities. Lose your stupid prejudice. Think of others first and your pride later.'

He just laughed. It was a hopeless situation. Eccentrics to start with, the whole atmosphere and excitement or dread of their discoveries made them impossible to argue with.

I was then thinking in terms of an invasion that was still to come. I did not realize fully that it was already happening.

3

The woman came about eight. Grey suddenly scaled the ladder back up into the hall of his living house. I followed him, though I had the feeling that both the girl and Potson might try and hold me back.

That was how frightened in my mind I was getting.

Laura, Maggy's mother, was like the girl, big, loose and voluptuous. From the look of her I thought Grey must have seduced her very early in life, for she looked around thirty-five. She was dark, with almost a Spanish look.

When Grey went forward to embrace her, she pushed him aside so that she could stare at me.

'Who's that?' she said.

He told her. I nodded and smiled. She smiled back. Yes, she was very much like her daughter.

'What goes on?' Grey said.

Slowly she turned her head from me to him.

'The only things anybody takes notice of is why people won't come here,' she said, and sat on a polished oak chest. 'But why is still in a Town Hall In tray. I saw the man and noticed one report had 'Smell' and a question mark scribbled on it. He said the demolition would go ahead when the compulsory notice had been served.'

'Is that all?'

'No. It seems they had trouble in some estate. When they were clearing the site they found an old burial ground, and old bones came up all over the place.' She laughed. 'They shifted it, but the first tenants found they'd got poltergeists and all sorts of hauntings. So they went. They've been empty since.'

'Auto suggestion,' Grey said contemptuously. 'It's just these people heard about the old bones and started imagining.'

She shrugged.

'Well, there's the fact. It's the reason why they don't bulldoze you right out now. They don't want another collection of empty lots.'

'Is that the delay?' he said.

'That's why they sent me, isn't it?' I said. 'Can't you remember anything?'

The grasshopper in his head was working overtime. The heat from the computer hall wasn't so bad upstairs, but the hum sensation still could be felt.

'You haven't eaten,' Laura said.

'No.' Grey was staring at nothing.

'I'll get something.'

She got off the chest and came by me.

'Come and talk to me,' she said.

I glanced at Grey, but he had turned and was on the point of going into his study. I followed her out into a kitchen. She started searching a fridge.

'Why did they send you?' she said.

'To find out what's wrong.'

'Oh, they know something's wrong, do they?'

'They're curious about why people won't come here any more. It was the car park, really.'

'That's the impression I got from the Council office,' she said. 'Superstition.

But why is a Ministry involved? Why are you here?'

I told her how I got lent around the different authorities. She didn't seem to listen between the smooth actions of getting a cold meal together.

'I don't live here,' she said. 'I come in because I know they don't eat unless I get them something. I don't live here. That's why I'm still almost sane.'

One couldn't miss the point.

'This thing has effects,' I said.

She laughed shortly.

'You don't know the half of it,' she said. She pointed towards the hall with a knife. 'He's always been an eccentric Irishman. But merry, cheerful, imaginative, sparkling. Not now. That's all gone. He's just plain mad. And Maggy. She rules them both. She's changed the least. It seems to affect the men most. They're getting fat. That lecturer is getting like a woman. It must be altering the glands somehow, as well as the brain cells. You might have called it a madhouse in normal times. But comparatively. Now it bloody well is one.'

'They don't want me to go,' I said.

'They won't let you go,' she said, spreading butter.

'But why? I could help in this. I could get the authorities — '

'The last thing he wants,' she said briskly.

'But what does he hope to do on his own?'

She looked up then and smoothed her hips with her flat hands.

'He hopes to let them in,' she said. 'Don't you understand what kind of madness this is? It's a sly, cunning, wicked madness that's come out of those bloody machines of his. He wants these things to come. He'd go raving mad if you tried to stop this happening.'

She laughed again and turned her back to go to the fridge. 'That's behind the mask,' she went on. 'What's on top may look mad, but it sounds almost reasonable, if you accept the fact that authority has played the hell with him for years. They've stolen from him, cheated him and bullied him when he complained. Carson isn't the steady, level headed character to let that go by.'

I tried to stop the distant hum and the heat from getting into my head and to think clearly about this. The woman could be right, but she could be quietly mad too. She might have some personal axe, such as having been neglected for this endless pursuit of experiment.

What she said could explain the otherwise inexplicable intention to keep me a prisoner.

'But surely you don't want these things to come?' I said.

I realize now that at this time, and in that weird air, I had accepted the fact of alien invasion before I had full knowledge that it had really happened. That was how strong the atmosphere was.

'What does it matter?' Laura said. 'The world is in a hell of a state through Men. Perhaps something else could be better in time. Certainly, it couldn't be worse.'

The idea that she might prove an ally for me evaporated.

'I shall have to go, you know,' I said. 'My office will start to wonder. Also my car is on the street.'

'The car will be towed away to a police

pound,' she said mixing dressing. 'Your office won't worry. You're on loan to somebody else and they closed long ago.' She went back to the fridge. 'And if you think of getting out this back way, there isn't one. All bricked in to make way for more machines.'

'You want me to stay, too?'

'I've lived with Carson on and off for twenty years. But on the average through that time, I want what he wants. This is as of now, too.'

I started to boil.

'I'm just an ordinary man from the Ministry,' I said. 'I came to make an investigation. Your husband — Grey told me everything, voluntarily. He showed me his proofs, told me what he expected. And now — '

'That's why he won't let you go,' she said. 'He wouldn't have told you if he hadn't been sure you couldn't tell anybody else. This is his, this affair. It's almost as if he's found admirers at last.'

Crazy, crazy. I had the idea of busting out, but I was not that far gone in the wild lands.

And anyhow, I wanted to stay. I wanted to know. If I learnt enough tonight, tomorrow was the important day to get help.

If it didn't happen tonight. If it did, it would be too late for help.

'Why do you want to go, anyway?' she said, slightly contemptuous. 'It's too late to do anything.'

I emptied out and felt sick.

'You almost read my thoughts,' I said.

'It isn't so difficult,' she said. 'You'll find that after a few hours in this place, what you think shows on your face. Once I told fortunes. Once when I left him. I knew nothing about it, but what I got from a book. But I told them in a tent on a seaside pier. After a while I could tell from their faces what they wanted to be told. You could say something, a probe, and watch the result. After that, you could go on.'

I wiped my face.

'It's getting hotter.'

'It isn't really heat. It's a kind of pressure. Sometimes it clings all round your face. Like being smothered. Like a lot of things fingering your face.'

She put it well, but she had been looking in on this nightmare for a long time, and had not been taken over completely, as the others had.

She pushed a plate of salad across the table to me.

'Eat it,' she said. 'You might not be getting anything more for quite a while.'

I ate a bit, but it was too hot and close to want much.

'So you think this thing is coming, do you?' I said.

'If you've got any sensitivity at all you can feel it is.' she said. 'It's like a pregnancy. The whole damned thing. Something building up that you can't stop without violence.'

'Do you think it will be violent?'

'If you can abort it will. If you can't it might be a smooth takeover.'

'You must have talked a lot about this.'

'Too much.'

'What does Grey really believe will come? Beings?'

'It must be something with intelligence, mustn't it? You can see the curve of the plot coming this way. It takes some artillery to make a shot like that.'

'Sometimes you talk like a journalist.'

'Why do you say that?' she smiled.

'I meet a lot in my job. Flower writers.'

'Thanks. I am one. That is how I can go and see the Council without them clamming up on me. They all jostle to get in front of the camera, these officials.'

'Are you writing this?'

She hesitated.

'I've written a lot. For myself. But it's ready if anything does happen.' She looked at my plate. 'Make an effort with that grub. You'll be grateful later.'

I tried. It turned to cork in my mouth. The heat and humming seemed to be growing. I said so.

'It isn't heat. I keep telling you. It's Genesis rearranging the molecules around. Fission. Shifting shapes. changing things makes heat. I got it all out of the library at the *News*.'

'Why didn't you ask the Science Correspondent? Hawkins. He's with it. Very much. He badgers me on nearly every job I get.'

'That's why. He'd smell out what was afoot.'

'Why are you keeping this secret?'

'Because Car isn't sure. The Things might miss. It's a big sky.'

'That isn't the reason. He was never frightened of failure. I know his record.'

'I told you. You obviously don't believe me. He wants them to come.'

'And you, too? To get a story?'

'You're incredulous. But then you're a practical man, and you want all human beings to be practical and logical according to the rules laid down by the lower IQ. You won't find any norms here, Richard. Except yourself, perhaps. And that won't last long.'

She watched me, as if she knew.

'It hasn't lasted this long,' I confessed. 'I keep getting nightmares. I fancied they would tear me apart. Perhaps eat me. I never thought of anything like that in my life before.'

'You will again. I know. There are two kinds of nerve drug. One kind that soothes you into drifting down a river of dreams. The other that sends you screaming over the rapids. This is the noisy one. We all get it.'

'How long since it started? This drugging?'

'You mean the radiation? About a fortnight, I suppose. When a thing starts it's light and easy and you take no notice. Then after it's got you by the throat you try and think when. But you didn't notice. I wish I had. It could have been coming on much longer. Infiltrating. It could have started with the desertion of the car park. But we don't know when that was either. Gradually people stopped coming. Suddenly somebody noticed the park was empty. Like that. But when did it start? Guess.'

'But the speed of the increase has been noticeable about a fortnight,' I said. 'Now it's outside. All round. Could it be that this invasion is actually on? After all they needn't be beings, monsters, anything tangible at all. There must be other forms of life besides the animal one. Other forms of intelligence.'

'What's the use of guessing?' She sounded exasperated all of a sudden.

'Why won't he get help?'

'You asked that before.'

'And got the wrong answer. I'm asking for another one.'

'He's scared, that's all.'

'Of these things?'

'No. Of authority. If they handed this thing over to the Defence Ministry, we'd get a war. War against something you know nothing about could slaughter everybody within hundreds of miles.'

'I've heard the theory before. But the Government isn't made up entirely of fools.'

'They're men, aren't they?'

I wiped my face again. As she said, the heat or whatever it was was like things feeling over your face, trying to stuff your nostrils with fingers and covering your mouth.

'Car is scared they'll fire off at something they can't hit. After all, that's natural, isn't it? To panic and shoot?'

'How does Grey know it can't be hit?'

'He doesn't. But he judges from the signs of the build-up that it'll be like that.'

'Do you know how much bigger this

star is they're coming from?'

'Much bigger than this.'

I got up and went to the window. The thick sky was fiery red over the black spires of the city. It looked ominous, but perhaps only because I knew something was going to happen.

'It's his duty to report it. Or let me.'

'Don't keep on,' she said, and lit a cigarette. 'You'll have to stay. He's mad on that theme. Since the development, nobody's got out again.'

She started then looked at me sharply. She hadn't meant to say it.

'Who came here before me?'

'A man. I don't know who. He complained he was getting interference from Car's apparatus. He knew a bit about it. That was the trouble.'

'Where is he?'

'Ask Car.'

'But this is incredible! You can't behave like this in the middle of a civilized city! What on earth does he think he's doing? I can't believe — '

'The whole thing is unbelievable,' she cut in. 'Small things like holding a man

hardly count against the fact that the
civilized city might disappear tonight.'

'That's as cracked as anything I've
heard yet! If that's what you believe, why
didn't you do anything? You were at the
Council this afternoon. You could have
warned them then.'

'What would they have done?' She
laughed shortly. 'They would have a
conference to decide whether I should be
certified mad or prosecuted as a public
nuisance. Or they might have thought
they should do something. What? Phone
your Ministry. What then? They'd send
you. Well, you're here now. So what more
could I have done?'

'But I could do a lot.'

'Enlarge.'

'I could get the whole radar networks
in action, every watch satellite looking
out, the space platforms on search — '

'And you would see it coming,' she
said. 'That's if it's not already here.
Didn't Car tell you? The nearer the things
get, so the radar and the telescopes lose
them.'

'Don't make it seem impossible.

There's always improvization.'

She waved her cigarette.

'Do you really think that if you got away from this atmosphere you'd be able to keep this stirring belief in alien invasion? I think you'd go, feel instant relief and that would make you think you'd been having a nightmare, been impregnated by an electronic needle in your mind.'

'I grant you I'd feel relief. But I've seen enough to convince me. It isn't just this radiated emotion. There's an obvious truth linking the vision from the scanners, the computers, the human checks — '

'Don't keep on.' She sounded tired. 'It's no damn good. Try if you like. But don't try too hard. Just give in when you fail.'

She smiled. I went out into the hall. Potson was sitting on the stairs morosely watching the front door. Maggy stood by the cloak chest riffling through a sheaf of loose papers she held in her left hand. She looked up when I came out, shaking her hair free from one eye. She looked at me with a big, loose smile.

To push on would be foolish. I felt the first wave of embarrassment at the thought of what must happen.

Potson turned his head to look at me. His fat shoulders shrugged very slightly, as if to indicate he could do nothing and neither could I.

Grey suddenly shouted from somewhere upstairs.

'New development. Come up! Bring that Ministry bug with you.'

Potson got up and turned to look up the stairs. I saw his face shining more brightly than his fat body, but with sweat not anti-radiation cream. Maggy threw the papers down on the chest and looked at me. Laura came out of the kitchen, stopped and looked up the stairs.

'What's happened?' she shouted in a tense, high pitched tone.

'Hell's rain!' Grey's voice came back. 'I don't know what. Come up!'

Potson started. Maggy nodded to me to go. I went. She came after me. As we ran up I glanced down over the banister.

Laura was standing down there, looking up. She wasn't coming. I got the feeling she was deliberately holding back from getting too much into the contamination rooms.

We went on up. Grey was in the scanner room, staring at the big colour scene on the wall. It was snowing golden sparks. They were being fired at us so realistically that I almost ducked until they flaked off distorted at the edges of the screen. There was so many we couldn't see what point they were coming from. They were swelling up so fast they hid the source of their coming.

'What the hell is it?' Maggy said.

'I'm guessing, too,' her father said. 'Somebody else have a penny on the drum.'

'How far out is this? The tube frame, I mean?'

'Ten thousand miles,' Grey said.

'So they could be big,' I said.

'Big as buses. Bigger,' Grey said. 'And they're coming up at some speed around fifty thousand. That's something.'

'This must be being picked up,' I said. 'They'll be coming in towards the watch satellites. They must be being tracked.'

'The splendid thing about my little

arrangement is it works on a far higher frequency range than anything that I know of. They need not register in the usual ranges. Look at this. Normal radio telescope transmission.'

He switched something over. The stars were there still, but much smaller, more indistinct. The general formation made the picture resemble the earlier, bigger version.

The golden rain had vanished. Everything was still in that night scene of depthless space.

He switched back again. The rain came on, furious, frightening.

'Is this the invasion?' I shouted.

He shrugged. I realized I had shouted because the humming in the house was growing louder, until I could actually feel it through the soles of my shoes.

The terror of the falling stars had let the humming go unnoticed until that moment of actual feeling.

Suddenly the rain stopped. The stars were still and undisturbed.

'That thing — there!' Grey suddenly yelled.

He ran round the scanner tables and to the great wall screen. He jabbed at the middle of the star scene with his finger.

We saw a small spot of light, which I would have taken for a distant star, but Grey jabbed it and shouted.

'That's new! It must be a launching platform! That's where they're coming from!'

'How far out is that?' I said.

'Too small to get a fix on,' he said. 'What would you make it, Maggy?'

'About half a mil,' she said, making jottings on a small pad. 'I should guess that from the time taken for the last lot of rain to travel to the frame and go over the edge.' She turned to Potson. 'Go and check with the tapes.'

Potson wiped his face and then went out and down the stairs.

'Well, there you are,' I said. 'It's on. You'd better let me do something now!'

'What?' Grey said.

'Don't keep saying what! I mean get Defence. Warn them. Get a reception ready. Preparation might save a lot of lives. Instead of sitting here inviting them — '

He ceased to listen and walked to the door.

'This is an interesting development,' he said. 'This changes the aspect of what I had thought. Come with me.'

I followed him downstairs and Maggy came after. He went to the front door. My heart speeded up then, but he turned with his hand on the lock and looked back towards the kitchen.

Laura stood there, watching him, big eyed, stiff with anxiety.

'What is it?' she said huskily.

'Them,' he said, and opened the door. 'I thought it would be tomorrow. All along I thought it would tomorrow.'

He stepped out and halted on the threshold. It was dusk, purple, smoky dusk, and the noise of the working city had gone. He stood there listening, but the humming inside the house was too strong to let us hear much else.

He looked back and nodded to me. Maggy slipped her arm through mine and held it tight, holding me, not from fear.

Potson came on the other side of me, but he was watching the sky. I did, too, but nothing was to be seen through the hot summer haze of the night.

We went out, across the road and on to the broken ground and flowering weeds of the bomb site. Then it came, the weird sound I had heard from the missile fragment. It could have been there before, but suddenly it was strong and rising in strength. Yet it was not a sound one heard through the ears. It was something getting right into the bones of the head. I tried jamming my ears with my hands, but the noises didn't diminish at all.

'Feel it?' Grey said.

He was tense then, his eyes shining in the dusk like those of a frightened black. The girl clutched my arm hard enough almost to paralyse the muscles.

'Oh Christ!' Potson moaned.

I couldn't make out what it was that was happening. My head felt hot and pressed as in a vice so that I couldn't think properly. The glow of the city in the sky was red and the occasional towers of flats and offices stood like stalks glittering with diamond lights.

There were no lights in Nelson Street, not even from the row of houses.

I looked at the scene to try and bring a normality into that foetid atmosphere and the rising panic of the sound.

'Listen, listen,' she hissed close to my ear. 'Flowers.'

I made no sense of what she said, and she kept on repeating it as if unaware that she was saying anything.

We kept looking at the sky, expecting the rain to show but the whole dome was still and void of stars.

'It's not there,' Potson said, bewildered. 'It's here. Now!'

But he didn't point anywhere, and seemed to be staring at nothing. His bare belly heaved with the panicky depth of his breathing.

The sound increased still more and the heat around us came like a blanket of smothering sensation. Sweat was running off my face.

The note began to undulate in waves of smoothly changing frequencies and some kind of harmonic began to respond from the ground we stood on. I looked at Grey. He stood knee deep in flowered weeds, his head turned upwards.

Realization came gradually. I saw the weeds moving as if touched by a wind, and then I realized the air was still. Yet the bells of the flowers waved and shook, nodding all round Grey.

I began to understand what she kept saying. The weeds were on the move. I looked all round me, and everywhere the tall weeds bobbed and waved as if suddenly come to life. I looked back to Grey. He still looked upwards.

The girl and Potson were staring at him, petrified, unable to move or say anything, but just stayed staring.

'Get out of there!'

I remember shouting suddenly and taking a step towards Grey, the girl dragging me back.

'No, no!' she said.

Grey looked down, startled by my shout. The weeds seemed to be reaching up at him, the leaves moving up above the flower heads like claws.

'Get out!' I shouted. 'They're all round you!'

He looked down and I saw him stagger back with the shock. Then his big head jerked round and he saw the waving, moving weeds in every direction, the movements making it seem that they marched like an army on the ground. It was mesmeric, for they must have stayed rooted.

Grey gave a sudden bellowing roar of alarm and trampled out of the weeds, breaking them down, brushing them aside. They seemed to claw at his legs as he went and the note of the undulating sound rose higher, almost into a screaming.

Maggy yelled something, trying to drag me back out of the ground of the weeds. The heat was rising from them, as if the bell mouths of the flowers exuded the smothering air.

Grey ran to the roadway like a charging elephant. I couldn't shake the girl off so I got her round the waist and just lifted her. Like that we staggered after Grey and as my legs brushed and broke the stems of the weeds I could hear the tiny screaming rising from their bells.

Once on the road I let her down. She was gasping, even sobbing with terror and tried to bury her face in my shoulder. She clung to me so that it hurt and kept gasping out flower names.

The sky was red, but the whole ragged field of the weeds was waving and glowing now with a red, luminous pale like smouldering fire.

I saw Potson still standing there amongst them this strange red glow shining on his fat, naked torso, gleaming on his sweating face and reflecting in red pools from his dark glasses.

'Potson!' I shouted. 'Come out!'

He stayed there, his arms down and outward from his sides, his hands dipped in amongst the waving weeds as if they had hold of his fingers and he could not move.

He began to go down on his knees, slowly, as if the tendrils pulled him down amongst them. Suddenly he cried out something and swept his arms round, gathering armfuls of the flowers to his chest. He stayed like that, on his knees, pressing the weeds to his breasts and shouting something I couldn't catch for the undulating screaming of the weeds.

'Get him out, for Christ's sake!' Grey bellowed and started forward.

Potson seemed to be dragged right down then, and he vanished in the ragged sea of weeds, yelling still.

Grey started trampling into the waving sea and the screaming grew higher, louder. I wrenched the girl from me and shoved her. As she went back I followed Grey into the moving mass of flowers.

Grey bent down and got hold of Potson. I saw him then, flower bells sucking on to his naked body like leeches, and tendrils wrapping round his fat arms.

I could feel them tearing at my legs, as if hundreds of them reached out and tried to catch me as the bells screamed up the frightful note. I could hardly see for sweat running into my eyes. It was like running through a mob of scratching, clawing dwarfs.

As we tried to pull Potson up, the flowers stuck to him and wound round our legs and arms like snakes. We pulled and tore to get him out of the yelling mass and as we trampled, stumbling out, Grey almost fell twice, pulled down by the weeds catching round his legs.

How the hell we got Potson out I don't know, with those awful things pulling and tearing at us, trying to get us down as they had got him down. The red luminous fire of the weed field was bright then, lighting us up as if we were reeling over the open griddles of hell.

When we got to the road, I went down and Potson came with me. I think Grey just let go and stood there, towering above us, panting and cursing, his face gleaming from the reflection of the red glow. Beyond him, a million miles up, the sky was purple-red, echoing the awful sound, but blank as a curtain over us.

Potson was gasping and grunting, stunned with terror.

'Get him into the house!' the girl shouted.

Grey came too. I got up and we bent to get Potson up again. It seemed essential to get out of that street then, as if the animated weeds might get up and chase us across the cobbles.

As we got him up I saw the end of the street by the light of the glowing flowers. There part of a fallen building had been left, narrowing the street entrance, and the weeds had planted themselves on the masonry and bricks. They were waving now across the gap reaching out, clawing, bells shaking, petals shivering in the weird light.

We got Potson into the house. Maggy slammed the door behind us and leaned against it, panting. There was a screaming inside the house too, a muffled, thin sound, but it made Grey start and rush into his study.

Laura and Maggy bathed Potson's face and body as he lolled in the chair where we put him. I went in to Grey.

He was bending by the old music cabinet. The door was open. He didn't say anything but backed so that I could see past him into the cabinet. The screaming was distinct, undulating, close to.

The piece of the rocket was writhing on

the shelf, moving like a soul in agony. He slammed the door, straightened and wiped his wet face. He looked at me, then went to the corner and filled a mug with black beer. He drank in a great gulp. I saw his hand shaking.

Laura came in the door.

'This isn't what you thought would come,' she said angrily.

'Did anybody?' he shouted.

He sat down at the table and stared out of the windows. I looked that way too, for the only light out there was the mad, waving glow of the weeds, and it was bright in the dark night.

'The things aren't coming,' Laura said. 'It's out there. That's been the trouble all the time. The weeds are infected. You've been picking up interference from under your own silly nose!'

He didn't say anything. Took another draught. Clearly, he wasn't sure himself then. But in that screaming heat it was almost impossible to think sanely at all.

Maggy came in.

'When's it going to stop, for God's

sake?' she screamed. 'When's it going to stop?'

She clapped her hands over her ears and bent her head as if sobbing.

'Look out the back,' I said, and pushed past the girl.

She turned and ran after me, I heard her gasping behind me as I went into the kitchen. I remembered that garden it looked down on, weed grown, a mad profusion of flowers and lord knows what all choked up together, growing high to reach the sun they were trying to choke each other from seeing.

The same animation was there, but the colour was different, some flame yellow glowing pools spotted the hot-coal pink, but the droning scream was going on there, too, and the vegetation was waving and clutching without cohesion, as if the plants tried to strangle each other.

The girl clutched me, her arms round my neck and started sobbing again.

'I don't want to look! Don't let me look!'

'For Christ's sake calm down a bit.' I

remember my voice grating with the dryness of fear as I stroked her back.

'Don't let them get in!' she cried suddenly. 'Don't let them get in!'

It was sheer nightmare. When she said that I got a sudden panicky fear that they might get in, under the doors, through cracks in the windows, up between the floor-boards.

My ears were then exhausted with the screaming, and with panic beating behind them I couldn't discern any difference in the night sound for a long time.

Laura came in.

'It's going down,' she said huskily. 'Going down.'

I listened then and realized she was right. The sound was dying. Very soon it became a murmuring, undulating still, but not screaming any more. The glow from the flowers almost died away, but they still moved, though more slowly, as if the madness had gone out of them.

But they still moved. They still moaned. Our relief wasn't all that great.

I heard Grey shout in the hall.

'Potson! Get down there. Run back the

tapes. Quick, man! Run back the tapes!'

Maggy eased off and let me go. I went past Laura and out to the hall. Grey was leaning against the front door watching Potson grunt and gasp his fat way down into the computer hall. As I stopped he reached the basement floor and waddled away to a control desk.

Grey came towards me.

'There might be something on those ribbons,' he said. 'We can check. Come on. We have to know.'

I followed him up the flights again. At that time I thought that what he had to know was the source of the star pictures he had got. If the golden rain effect had been a trick pick-up from the energized flowers, an edge radiation, it could be analyzed and the cause of this nightmare explained.

It was nice to think on those lines, for with all the horror and the terror of the mad weeds, they were, after all, known species. They could be matched some-how, once it was known what had taken hold of them.

It was easier to deal with than an

unknown which might come in from far outside.

In the radar room the big scene was still on the screen, the watch on space, the stars, the calm, frightening depth of the void, as if one could drown mentally from the sheer vastness. I felt that then, but I was worked up to a state where I could feel any nightmare was real.

He flicked the scene off.

'Coming on now,' Potson's voice said through a speaker.

His voice was replaced by the wandering whistling and mush sounds of space coming from the tapes. The signal echoes from distant stars and space wanderers was familiar enough to bring me a feeling almost of peace. But that, too, had the effect of vastness somehow, of stereoscopic depth where one could drown once more.

The picture came up on the screen. It looked exactly the same as the one Grey had just switched off. It was. An hour's difference in space is the same time, as near as makes no difference.

The last of the golden rain was flying

off the edge of the screen in this replay. After that, all was still again.

The sound tape was interrupted sometimes by the crackle and hum of some far out interference, some gatecrashing signal from the depths.

In one corner of the picture was a ghost clock with second sweep circling continuously.

'You're too far back,' Grey shouted into a mike. 'Jump it.'

The sound screamed and made me jump, let alone the tape. The scene was unaffected.

Waiting, nervous, riding the nightmare, yet still something struck me about that picture which was stranger than the normal.

I had seen many such projections, black and white, full normal colour, infra-red colour, cobalt filtered, all one-colour reduced, spectrum screened, but I had never seen such a perfect picture anywhere, any time, as this jumped-up speciality in a broken down house in the middle of a disaster area. It was perfect. It had a fusion of colour I had never seen.

In fact it gave the impression that the colours were not of this world at all but a mixture produced by a different atmosphere altogether.

'How do you get this colour?' I said while the tape was chattering.

'Normal systems that. It's the receiver which is mine.'

'You never saw colour like that on any other tube.'

'No other feed to the tube is the same. All feeds start at the beginning.' He wiped his face. It was running with sweat.

We watched. There was only stillness to watch. Once a star fell, streaking down into nothing far out in nowhere. It was almost a shock.

'That'll be us one day,' Grey said.

The atmosphere made one feel that the final tragedy could be tomorrow, not a few million years hence.

The tape slowed down again. The old space mush came in. The ghost clock, which had spun fast, steadied to normal.

It began as a distant whisper, then grew clearer. The same eerie undulating wail that had now grown so terribly familiar.

He looked at me sharply, his eyes gleaming.

The sound went on, faint in the background, but unmistakeably the same.

'Was that a catch of the sound out there?' I said, pointing to the stairs.

'Impossible,' he said. 'The catch is as far out as the picture base. Ten thousand miles. The sound's out there — ' he pointed to the screen, ' — right out there!'

'Then it can't be sound.'

'No. It's electronic dissonance. But it's a transmission all the same. A signal being beamed in here, linking with the original source of the contamination out in the bomb site.'

'It must be a transmission of energy,' I said. 'The weeds couldn't act like they did without direct energisation.'

'You may be right. I don't know. There could be a sympathetic response in vegetable structure which reacts to this signal. That's possible, too.'

'Whatever it is,' I said, 'we must get help now. If this effect spreads God knows what it might do.'

'It could spread,' he said, wiping his face again. 'Yes, I think you're right now. You'd better go get help. Tell them.'

I should have collapsed inside with the relief at his change, but I didn't. Instead I got such a feeling of dread at the idea of leaving that house that my stomach quailed.

4

The night was murmuring when I left the front door. The weeds were moving still, and glowing too, but there was a softness in the action now, as if they were watching me.

Grey stood behind me. I looked back at him, my heart thumping.

'Too late,' he said.

That was all. I looked down Nelson Street. The old broken surface had been almost crumbled like pie crust, and up through the gashes the weeds stood, waving slowly, waiting for me.

The other end of the street they had covered the heap of fallen masonry, pushed up through the cracks in the old roadway and reached the housefronts. The murmuring was like a storm in the distance.

Sheer panic ran in me and I shut my eyes to try and control it. When I opened them again they filled with sweat. I wiped them with my hands and looked at the encroaching weeds.

'How are they growing at such a rate — spreading — ' I remember I had to say that twice because the first time my throat was so dry with fear the sound almost wasn't there.

'Something evil, man. Evil,' Grey said. 'I never thought of this. You can't go through there. They'll get you like Potson. They'd have strangled him, maybe eaten him. These things aren't natural any more. Something's using their fibres like mechanical limbs. That's what it is. Their nature is being speeded, distorted, used.'

'Why on us?' Maggy shouted from behind him.

'You asked for it,' I said, going back up the step. 'You signalled. You encouraged the heat and the sound. You kept it warm and secret so that now you've got it, but it's cut you off from help.'

'There may be a way at the back,' Laura said. 'There just may be.'

She covered her face with her hands a moment, then dropped them again.

'You can see from the landing window,' she went on.

I went in, past Maggy and Grey. They stood there staring out at the weed world, watching the things creeping up through new cracks in the roadway.

Laura came with me to the stairs.

'The top landing. You can see all the gardens from there.'

I ran up. She came after. At the top landing I unbarred the shutters and unfolded them. They groaned. They hadn't been undone for months. I shoved the window open and leaned out.

The gardens were wild seas of weeds and flowers, all moving with that strange, slow dancelike motion. Then something caught my eye on the wall below me.

A whole sheet of creeper was moving against the wall, climbing up towards me. I jumped back before I realized it had many feet to go to reach me.

'What is it?' she said, close behind me.

'Japonica,' I said. 'Crawling up the ruddy wall like a bloodstain.'

'But why? Why all this? In a derelict place with only us here?'

'The place is derelict because the rocket landed here, and laid the contamination. For all we know these weeds have been sucking in that contamination generation after generation for years back. Perhaps they aren't weeds we know any more. The trouble is nobody ever bothered to look. Few people study weeds, and if they do they don't choose bombsite car parks. The authorities knew there was something weird here, but they didn't think of weeds. Weeds are something you burn up.'

'Couldn't we do that?'

'How? Where would we find a flame thrower? Why didn't you have the phone?'

'He tore it out.'

'He's crazy. With all this electronic equipment, hasn't he got a radio transmitter that could hitch on to a police band?'

'I don't know. Wait.'

She leant over and called down the stairs.

'Yes!' I heard Grey shout in sudden excitement. 'There isn't one, but we could make a hook-up.'

'How long will it take?' I bellowed. 'These things are crawling quicker than you think!'

'An hour. Maybe two.' He was panting out words as he thundered up the stairs towards us. 'Have to sort out — old junk.'

We followed him through the radar room. The screen was blazing golden rain again. He stopped, staring at it.

'It's coming,' he croaked. 'It must be. The weeds — they must be a sort of preparation. Blanket barrage. Something.'

'What are they?' Laura said.

'Giant beans,' said Grey, staring. 'They land here outside. Up shoots a mighty beanstalk. Ten thousand miles high. Down climb the bug-eyed monsters . . . '

He went into the next room, still talking and switched on lights. These rooms had been joined together just by knocking holes through the partitions. He marched through about three and came into a glory hole of a workshop. Everything was all over the place, radio stuff, electrics, bolts, test tubes, cables, the lot, all as mad as he was.

My heart sank. If he was to make

anything out of this confusion of junk it would take not one hour, or two, but several.

His idea of grudging society and cutting himself off from it was paying him back now. He had just no means in that place of communicating with the outside world, something he now needed. To hell with them, he had said. Now it was to hell with him and the lot of us.

It was a pity Laura hadn't lived with him. She would have had the phone put back.

He started rummaging. I went on through to the end room. There was a window, boarded up. I got my fingers round a plank and pulled against the rusty nails. It hurt, but it suddenly gave and I peered out of the gap.

It was a dormer, and the slate slope ended in a gutter just below the window. I pulled out another couple of planks and got out on to the roof.

I looked down on the car park, the roadway where the tumbled masonry straggled like a headland, the empty space where the houses ended and ran on towards the derelict, boarded-up little houses that once had formed the neighbourhood.

Everywhere the weeds were moving. It was like a glowing sea, gathering round the lost terrace of houses where we were.

Peering directly down I saw the weeds growing high, seeding in the rotten powdery mortar between the bricks and coming up that way.

Laura looked through the broken window.

'What's happening?'

I didn't say.

'We might signal from here with a lamp,' I said. 'Is there such a thing? Powerful torch?'

'Why? Can you see anybody down there?' she said, suddenly breathless with excited hope.

'No.'

She went back. I kept watching and hoping somebody might come near, but the derelict area was bigger than I had thought. Far bigger.

Laura came to the window again, Maggy beside her. Their pale faces looked ghastly from the distant lights of the city.

'Will this do?'

She handed out a small pocket torch with a lens like a pea.

'No.'

'It's the only one.'

I leaned on the roof slope and just stared out towards the City. So near, so far. I clambered back in. Both women watched me.

'Will we ever get out?' Maggy said.

'If we can get a word through.'

We went back into the workshop, where Grey was cursing as he searched for something amongst his junk. Potson was there scratching his fat belly with the corner of a paper.

'They can't be coming straight in,' he said, looking towards us suddenly, as if we were invaders. 'The calculations make they should be here by now. They must be hanging up somewhere out there.'

'Why? Waiting for the weeds to devour us first?'

'That would be a way, wouldn't it?' Potson said, his glasses gleaming in the light. 'Use the vegetation, animated to choke and destroy opposition. Then come in and reverse the process which animated them. Like sending in a ferret to make the rabbit run.'

'The ferret kills the rabbit,' said Grey, still searching. 'Where's that bloody pack of transistors?'

'If you think this is the subject of an invasion experiment,' I said, 'isn't it stupid for the aliens to give such a game away on a small scale like this?'

'You don't know how many damn places this is happening in do you?' Grey said.

'We should have heard,' I said. 'These days we're pretty jumpy about unusual things happening. Side effects can produce hell all of a sudden.'

'Well, you didn't jump on this one, did you?' he bawled. 'You came because somebody thought something was wrong. That's all. You didn't track anything. It tracked you. That could have happened in a dozen places. Everywhere that ruddy rockets have landed in the last thirty years. Have you thought of that?'

'You mean space capsules?'

'No, I mean old rockets, first and second stage cans that go on whirling round like a lot of dustbins out there and finally come in and break up. That's the sort I mean. The others are checked. The dustbins aren't. They come in, burn up, bits fall, no matter how small, contamination. They land anywhere, wheatfields, steppes, paddy fields, the sea, cities, green belts — bits so small they're never noticed. The germs. Like the ones outside here now. How many places in the world have they landed? . . . Where are those — ah! thank the lord!'

He grabbed a box out of a mass of rubbish and went to an overloaded bench.

Potson said: 'They're standing out there.'

'You said that already!' Maggy cried out.

'We've got to realize it, haven't we?' Potson said. 'They hurt, those weeds. They bit me.'

He rubbed his belly again.

'They would have eaten me,' he went on, staring. 'But they can't. What with?

You can't without any teeth.'

'They can suck you to bits,' Grey said. 'Plug in that iron and don't blabber.'

Potson plugged the iron in.

'Suppose they get in?' he said.

He sounded almost vague, as if he didn't care much either way. Perhaps shock had unhinged him, specially after the tense atmosphere in this hell hole of a house.

'Nobody's watching the screen!' Grey bellowed. 'Get in there somebody. Are the tapes running, Potson?'

'They never stop,' Potson said. 'Miles and miles of tape and we don't understand a bloody inch. It makes you sick.'

Maggy went by and through to the radar rooms. She almost shouldered Potson aside, she was so mad with him. At any other time I might have thought that being that mad, she might have cared for the fat chump.

'If we could read them,' Potson yelled in his high woman's voice, 'we wouldn't be here now, standing like rabbits to a snake. Remember the square on the hypotenuse. It's got to equal the squares on the other two. Got to.'

'Jesus Christ!' said Grey, exasperated. 'Cork that blow hole somebody.' He knocked over a pile of cable reels. They thumped down and started to roll in radials, unreeling wire.

'It would be all right if it wasn't so hot!' Potson shouted. 'But you can't breathe.'

'Get down on those tapes!' Grey snarled.

'What's the good?' Potson said. 'We can't read them. We don't understand what they're saying.'

'Get out of my way!' Grey bawled.

Potson just stood there.

'They're standing out there,' he said, pointing to the rotten ceiling.

Grey ignored him and got on with his haphazard work.

Potson turned and went through into the radar room. I followed a little way behind him. He didn't see me. He went up to Maggy and grabbed her by the arm, turning her to face him.

'You fat ape!' she said.

'You got me here,' he said, his high

voice trembling. 'I'd be out there alive, like I used to be. It was you. You dragged me. You did it. A trap. You fooled me!'

'You fooled yourself!' she cried back. 'However did you kid yourself any girl could really fall for you? How — '

'Bitch! Bitch!' He screamed at her then let her go, shoving her aside as he did it. He blundered on, thighs knocking the radar pans as if he could not see. When he got out to the landing I heard him sobbing.

He had broken up.

She stood rubbing her hurt arm and looking at me with that one eye, her hair swinging as she breathed hard in a rage.

Then her eye switched to someone beside me. Laura. I had not heard her for the shouting and the humming of the massed electrics.

'You're a fool, Maggy,' Laura said, angrily. She followed Potson out.

Maggy turned her back on me quite suddenly. On the screen beyond her the golden rain had stopped again.

'What the hell is that stuff?' she said. She sounded angry and shaky now, as if it was getting her, or Potson was, or just everything was.

'Something being fired,' I said. 'That's my guess. But why does it splay out, if it's aimed at us?'

'Could be curving round to get us from behind as well,' she said. 'It's been all curves. Enough to curve your mind, too.'

'If they're being fired, they've got some way of stopping in mid-action or they'd have been here by now.' The scene amid the stars was still. 'Can we blow up that platform of whatever it is your father pointed out?'

'You've got top magnification now. Can do no more.'

There was a shout from downstairs. I thought it was Laura, but when I went out and looked down over the rails, Potson was running up.

'The computers! Get Grey! Quick!'

He turned to go down again.

'What's the matter?' I shouted down.

The girl came to my shoulder and looked down, holding her hair aside. Potson hesitated, looking up.

'They're coming alive!' he croaked.

Then he went on down. I heard Laura shout something, and I started to run down. Maggy went back into the top rooms.

At the bottom Potson was standing in the hall, his back against the far wall, looking down the broken wall to the hall of the machines. Laura was standing holding the newel post, looking at me.

'They're alive,' she said. 'What the hell are we going to do?'

The hall was humming madly. The very air trembled with it and the heat and smell of electrics was apalling, gushing out of the opening like an open fire door. Only a few lights still burnt in that long makeshift hall, but by it I could see steel cabinets moving like robots, bumping against each other, turning, like a lot of blind monsters. Every light on them that should have shown merely glowed ember red. The tapes were whizzing, screaming as they went.

'I've cut every switch in the place but just those lights,' Potson said. He grinned as if all his teeth ached. 'There's no juice on down there. None at all. Look at 'em!'

111

The crashing, clatter, humming and screaming made a din that made the floor shake.

Suddenly I found Grey beside me, staring down, petrified. He moved just to wipe his sweating face with an open hand and that was all. Potson shook with every crash of the wandering machines below, as if they bumped him.

'It's the shaking makes them walk,' Grey said at last. 'The floor's shaking down there. It'll crack soon.'

He was beyond any stage of dramatics. He just said things flatly, with no emphasis at all.

'Why is it shaking?' I said. I went to the street door and swung it open.

The weeds waved now from every crack in the tarmac, every joint in the old cobbled places which had never been tarred over I saw cobblestones being pushed up, as if giants were shoving up from underneath, being forced up by the gathering masses of the weed roots swelling between them.

The car park was now a moving mass of them, and the old buildings on the other sides of it were being engulfed by rising masses of the weeds. They were seeding in the walls, climbing up, crumbling out the old mortar to get a footing.

'What will ever get through that lot?' I said. 'Fire's the only thing and we're in the middle of it.'

'If this is happening in many places over the world,' Grey said. 'warning signals must be being sent out. It will wake somebody.'

'Get that radio working,' I said. 'At least there is a hope there.'

'Dear Sir, we are surrounded by anthropomorphic weeds, please send a fire engine, flame thrower, squadron of tanks and helicopters.' Potson laughed wildly as he ended.

Grey just went on up the stairs.

'And the computers are waltzing. Don't forget that!' Potson bawled after him. 'Please send also some anti-waltz powder for hysterical automated adders and square their hypotenuses — '

'Shut up!' Maggy squealed.

Potson did. He opened the door of the

study behind him and went into the room.

'Make some tea!' he shouted back. 'That cures everything.' We heard him laughing even above the thundering din of the machines.

Down there they were bumping and crashing, wheeling, blind, shattering their insides with every clanging crash.

But their lights glowed still, and the tapes were screaming round. Even as I watched one burst out from behind the glass and shot away trailing tape through the air like a streamer.

'Where are they getting the juice from?' I said.

'The heat in the metal?' the girl suggested.

'Must be some heat,' I said. 'But if the metal atoms are being changed that might generate enough electric heat to work something. It's all guesswork now. They've got something we've never heard of.'

'Helicopters!' Potson shouted from in the room. 'Ask for helicopters. It's the only way we'll ever get out of this hellhole.'

'We haven't got a line yet,' I said. 'It'll keep.'

Maggy slammed the door again. Nobody liked that wild scene. Not that it was much worse than the death dance of the mad machines. The whole lot was a screaming nightmare. I felt then it would be lucky if we stayed sane much longer.

Or were we sane then?

'Why don't they stop?' Laura came and screamed in my ear above the unholy din.

'The whole floor's trembling down there. And the machines. They must have got it. Same as the weeds. Same as that bit of rocket in there. Writhing. Twisting up. If the floor's got it, won't the walls start, too?'

'The whole bloody place will collapse!' Maggy cut in.

Then suddenly the machines stopped. The silence was terrifying, as if all our senses had stopped working and we were left with just a still picture of what we had last seen on our retinas.

'Did that do it?'

Grey's voice bawled down from the top landing.

'It's stopped!' I shouted back. 'What have you done?'

Potson came running out of the study and stopped in the doorway, stunned by the sudden quiet of the machines.

'I switched off the radar!' Grey shouted. 'The animation must be coming in on the beam, living in the echo and feeding straight into the recording boxes down there. I just thought of it!'

Maggy ran to the door and opened it.

'The weeds're still moving!' she said huskily.

'They must be different from the machines,' I said. 'But there's a clue here somewhere.'

Maggy shut the door quickly. I knew that she was frightened that the damned things would start marching up the steps and into the house. They looked as if they could.

The stoppage of the machines eased the tension somewhat. The loss of the noise made the difference. In the easement it was Laura who took the lead.

'There are all sorts of possibilities,' she said. 'That we'll die somehow, or some

116

things will come that will hurt us. That the house will collapse. I don't deny any of these things. I'll just point out that there is one more possibility that nobody seems to have counted.

'The possibility that we might get out of here. That's the one we ought to keep in mind. Everything's frightening that we don't understand. All the unknowns are monsters until you meet them. Hysteria doesn't help us. If these things are like animals, they'll smell fear and they'll hate it and try to kill it.

'We all keep thinking this weed contamination and the machines dancing about is some malign thing being sent down. Suppose it isn't? Suppose it's a side-effect from some kind of radio they're using. Nothing more than that? Suppose they're not invading, but trying to get in touch? There may be all sorts of explanations to these things — '

'They tried to eat me,' Potson said. He spoke quietly, which after his hysterical manner before, seemed to make his words all the more terrifying.

'That still doesn't mean they're malignant,' Laura protested. 'Fear could have made you think that because we've never seen such a thing before. But they move, so you immediately think of fly-eating, bird-eating plants. Horrors of nature. They come first to the mind and persuade you — '

'You wouldn't go out there,' Potson said quietly.

'No,' she said. 'Not till I understood more about what's going on. That's what we ought to do until Car's finished that radio. Try and find out what's really happening. God knows, we should have enough to go on by now.'

Potson sat down on a chair by the front door. He even relaxed quite a bit, though he was still quick and nervous when he spoke.

'Enough to go on, to add up. But how do you add up when you don't know what the figures mean?'

'There must be a clue to it,' Laura said.

'The calculations of the curves all agreed, the time, the angles, everything came out right whichever way we worked it. They didn't keep secret that they were coming. We plotted that, but the ordinary radar belts don't hitch on to these golden things. They just don't. So these things must know the usual frequencies we use in this planet. How would they blank that off?'

'They could be using re-senders,' I said. 'They get the radar transmission and retransmit it on so that no echo comes back to the receivers. But obviously they haven't hitched on to Grey's frequency yet. When they do, the echoes will disappear from that as well.'

'At any rate, they're using a form of radio that's like our normal ones,' Laura said.

'They're using it to blank our radar,' I said. 'But that doesn't mean they use that form for their own communications. In fact, the way the weeds work and the metals jangle it could be something very different.'

'I wish those damn weeds would die!' Maggy cried out.

That brought another silence. For one awful moment I thought Laura would suggest making tea and bring the whole new build-up of sense crashing to the ground. Perhaps she had too much sense.

Through the closed door we could hear the whispering of the weeds, talking together, discussing which way to get in.

I must have laughed for Maggy turned on me.

'What's the matter?' she said.

'A thought,' I said. 'Mad. I'm going to look out. Just in case something comes near.'

'What will?' Laura said. 'This is desolate. That's one way to drive him out, make him sell, your council thought. Isolate him. They probably didn't think that could be what he wanted. They won't leave people alone. They won't leave people to be alone. Save him. Give him people. Sandbag him with talk he doesn't want to hear. Company. The need of the nitwit.'

She went on talking as I climbed the stairs. The radar room was still, not humming any more. It seemed peaceful, not so frightening. Grey was still working in one of the lighted rooms beyond. It was like going through a tunnel made of broken walls to reach him.

'Soon?' I said.

He just nodded. I went to the room where I had unboarded the window and clambered through to the parapet again.

Looking at the sky, and the glowing city, it was all serene, quiet, the town noises remote, a far, soft background.

But down below the whispering, waving weeds still moved, laughing up at me, a sea now, clambering walls and covering ground like an army swelling out from a forgotten perimeter.

Their glow was dull, but still the field of the one time car park was like a red, slowly smouldering fire.

Grey came to the opening behind me. He had a telephone in his hand.

'Hooked up,' he said. 'They won't take me for serious. Police. You take it.'

The line was full of mush and crackle, but it was working. Grey had got on to a police station, the nearest one, I supposed but didn't wait to find out.

'I want a line to The Science Ministry,' I said. 'Urgent immediate.' I gave the listener my identification number. He spoke to somebody and then clacked into action.

The Ministry came through.

'Sir James Harcourt,' I said. 'Can you find him?'

'He's in his office. I'll ring him.'

If Harcourt was in his office instead of dining with some foreign contact, something must have happened. When he answered I just told him flat what the situation was.

'What do you want? Flame throwers?'

'We'd be in the middle,' I said. 'I want a couple of tankers full of weed killer and a half dozen fire engines to pump it.'

'Where in hell am I going to get two tankers at this time of night?'

'There's Alifex. They keep big stocks.'

'That's way out in Hertfordshire!'

'We can wait if you get on quick. They could be here in an hour.'

'If we got contact. Hang on. I want to talk to you.' I heard him giving orders to get Alifex, snapping it out. He came back. 'They'll try. There may be nobody at the storage plant. Just give me that description again. I have a tape here.'

I told him about the weeds, the machines, the golden rain, and Grey's outlandish frequency which was temporarily foxing the re-senders.

'We're getting reports of disturbances from several places,' Harcourt said. 'That's why I came back here. Stories of wheatfields waving about. People watching. Flowers walking about. I didn't believe a damn thing till you came on. We'd better check up the others pretty quick.'

'What do they think it is — the ones watching?'

'They think it's a side-effect of pesticides.'

'I hadn't thought of that one! Remember that Walkura stuff that made the weeds wriggle about? That was a year or two back. I'd forgotten it. Been too damn scared to remember.'

'Couldn't it be that?'

'What about the machines?'

'If you've got too high frequencies in that house, you could be having overheating from that. It's a possibility.'

'What about the golden rain?'

'How do you know the radar's actually seeing that stuff? He's using a system nobody's tried before. It could have its own fits. After all, it is amateur and untried.'

'You're killing the legend.'

'I have to be responsible. No other radar in the world is tracking anything. Why should just one? Especially as you're getting explainable reactions to super high frequencies.'

'You ought to be here. This is no uhf effect. This is something alive.'

'Yes, but apart from the weed killer, what do you expect me to do? What I've just said to you will be said to me from every department if I take your line. You know that.'

'This is the very attitude Grey was scared of!'

'Be sensible! I have to deal with Government departments. They don't believe in miracles. They believe in side-effects.'

Harcourt shook me back on my heels. I realized then that from the start I had thought only along one line, the line that Grey had given me. That was not my usual way of behaving.

It was my job always to find out. What I had done here was to be told what I was supposed to find out. The penetrating atmosphere and the madness of the three people had gathered me into their way of thinking.

But I leaned there against the slated slope and stared down at the moving field of the massed weeds and horror drove me back into Grey's mental arms again.

'It can't be side effects,' I said. 'It just can't be. It's too powerful altogether! That radar was too perfect to be wrong!'

'So the other twenty thousand perfect and *proved* ones are wrong and this one right? Who can I tell that to, apart from Marines? Grey's reputation as a steady character just doesn't exist. He's a flash-in-the-pan strike-it-lucky-sometimes electronics weirdie. Maybe he's dead right. Who am I going to get to believe it when all the other watchers say he's wrong?'

'Like I said, the re-senders — '

'All right then why haven't the satellites got anything? Or the space platforms? They haven't reported anything. They could see with their TV, even if the radar was jammed.'

'If you think blank like this, why bother to send the weed killer?' I shouted at him.

'Because we must get you out of there before they make the house collapse,' he said. 'That seems to me the main and only danger if they're rooting in the mortar between the bricks it's bound to crack the building up sooner or later. Watch a bit of groundsel come up and crack six inch concrete. You know how it happens.'

He was speaking to me as if I were a gentle lunatic who might boil up, or a child holding an open razor.

In that place, in those conditions it was impossible to be sane. But he, faraway from danger could be sane.

'When he turned off his radar, the machines stopped,' he said. 'Isn't that a direct clue? The uhf was energizing the machines. By induction. We don't fully know the effects of uhf multiplied by laser, multiplied by lord knows what. It might produce anything. Even enough energy to drive cars from a central station, just by induction. Remember Arvin Motors are working on that now. They burnt a field of barley out with radiation.'

'This isn't the same at all. It isn't the same! Listen. Get that helicopter over. Get the others off the roof — '

'Why not you?'

'I'll wait for the weedkiller. I want to save this radar. It's got to be saved somehow.'

'I've already laid on the chopper,' he said. 'A service one. It should be over in a half hour. There wasn't a duty flight nearer than Portsmouth. There'll be two. One coming to look, take the pictures of this weed. They'd have been there sooner only there has been a big explosion in the sea off the Isle of Wight. Could be an aircraft gone in. So far they can't find any wreckage.'

'When was this?'

'Not long before you rang.'

'Any radar track of it?'

He laughed quietly. 'No. But often there isn't if it's low. Also, it could have been a drifter mine. They're still about.'

The mush hissed in my ear.

'Keep this line on,' he said, and cut off his end.

I looked back into the window. Grey was standing there holding an earpiece. He had heard the lot.

'An ironic situation,' he said. 'First we imprison you, then when you're free, you won't go. More, you came here persuading me of the excellence of your departments and their ways of thinking. Now you come to my point of view. You suffer as I did.'

I let him go on and stood there leaning against the slope. Far off a jet made an approach. Its distance away seemed to emphasize the loneliness of this place.

'Do you know anything that will change his mind?' I said.

'He's doing what he can for you, within the limits of his incredulous mind. Who do you think will take the lift?'

'The lot of you.'

'I'll wager you nobody goes,' he said.

Laura appeared beside him and pushed out a mug. I drank some hot tea and felt better.

'There's a chopper coming to lift you off,' I told her.

'Maggy won't go,' she said.

'Why not?'

'I know she just won't. Who plans to go?'

'I'm waiting here,' Grey said. 'It might do some good. We have a line now. We can tell them what's going on. They might find something that can be done.'

'What about the weed killer?'

'You might make a path through them. You couldn't kill the lot. Take a look round. It's gone too far. It's out of hand.'

I could feel the roof trembling a little under my feet. They were getting in the cracks down below, and there was still the deep humming from the ground which was as much vibration as aural.

'You don't think the women will go?'

'I know they won't go. Bloodyminded lot.'

'The houses might collapse.'

'They might fall off a helicopter. What's

129

the choice? Might. But Potson's sure to choose the devil he knows.'

He wouldn't go anyway, unless Maggy went, too.

'I wish you hadn't taken so much bloody trouble to isolate yourself here!' I shouted at him.

'So do I — now,' he said. 'I just didn't think it would be like this. I didn't think it would start down here. I thought something would have to land.'

I looked at the great pool of lightless desolation which the rocket had first created, and which Grey, with his obstinacy, kept a desert because it wasn't worth anybody coming in until they got control of his property in the middle. It was incredible to look down on this isolation close to a city's heart and to think that it had been held and extended by one determined man. There was, after all, something in social compulsion.

Harcourt came through suddenly.

'There's been another marine explosion, off Plymouth. It can't be aircraft. There's no radar track of anything coming in. What about Grey's detectors?

Can he see anything?'

'They're out. They made the machines dance.'

'Get him to try again. It's strange, two explosions and no trace afterwards.'

'Anybody seen anything? Coastguards?' I said.

'They reported the explosions. They don't mention anything coming down. Just a minute. Hang on . . . '

I heard him bark something, and then there was a clattering of a quick voice on some phone.

'Harcourt wants the radar on again,' I said back to the window.

'I heard. What are these things? Must be the rain we saw.'

'Well, go and try again. See if there's anything on your blippers.'

He shrugged and went away. Then I thought of the machines down in the basements. The house was already murmuring with the spread of weed life that was trying to wreck it. The rumbling thunder of the machines again might bring the moment of collapse much nearer. My stomach emptied into a void and I started sweating ice again.

I knew just when he switched on. The vibration of the machines ran in the structure under my feet like some kind of massage tickler. I pressed back against the warm slates as if something was trying to push me forward over the parapet and down into the weeds.

'Richard?' Harcourt came in again. I grated out some answer. It hurt my throat. 'There's more of these damn things. At intervals round the coast. Off Lundy. One off Cardiff. That's four. But no radar trace. Is he trying?'

'Yes, he's trying.'

'Well he — ' He broke off and I heard the clattery voice again. 'Off Harwich now. It's an enclosure working out. Encirclement. Why here? There's no reports of any anywhere else.'

'You've got to start somewhere. This is the place that got the V2s. What about Russia?'

'The Russians never admit anything. Specially if they can't track it.'

Laura came to the window.

'Car says come back and look.'

I got back in the window, bringing the phone on its long cable. It ran right back to the workbench in another room and could just go on into the radar room.

Everything was working, humming, blazing and shaking from the waltzing matildas in the basement. The house felt like a ship vibrating from wild sea and a Diesel engine that is breaking up.

The big scene on the wall was normal now, watching the moon instead of peering at stars right beyond it. Grey pointed. There was something crossing the pocked face of the moon. It crossed at an acute angle for its size increased at a frightening pace.

'It's coming towards us!' I remember shouting, as if everybody else didn't see that, too.

The thing swelled up and skimmed by on the left upper corner of the screen. I wiped my face and told what I had seen into the phone.

'What did it look like? What is it?' Harcourt cried.

'It didn't get close enough. Looked like a fat disc, but it moved too fast and too far off to be sure.'

Then Potson spoke from the other side of the room. He had a pad and pencil clutched to his fat chest. He looked up from it.

'From the grid reference on screen it should land two degs East, twenty North.' he said.

'Say again,' Harcourt said as I repeated what Potson said. 'I'll check with the wall map.'

I said again. Harcourt grunted.

'Three miles off Flamborough Head. Get them, will you? Fylingdales, Flamborough lookout.' He shouted to someone offstage. 'How far out when you saw it?'

I asked Potson.

'Fifty thousand,' he said.

'Can you back track and catch it again?' I shouted to Grey.

'Okay but there's another one coming. Look.'

Something seemed to come directly out of the face of the moon, swelling up at incredible speed.

'How far is that from camera?' I said.

The place was shuddering. I heard

Laura gasp and saw her clutch one of the scanning pans to steady herself.

'It's the chopper on top of us!' Maggy cried out.

'How far from camera?'

'When spotted, a hundred miles,' Potson said.

The thing swelled and whizzed over the top of the screen. Carson started turning wheels on a control panel. We drew back from the moon as if flying backwards through dizzy space. We came right back until the thing was overhead like an aircraft hovering while the stars rushed by and down into the vastness behind the moon.

'It's a disc. Going like hell,' I said.

'We're coming back scale speed a hundred thousand knots, holding it steady,' Potson said. Now he had figures to work out his shakiness had gone. Only breathlessness remained.

'A hundred thousand,' Harcourt said. 'That's a bucketful of knots . . . All defence systems now alerted red . . . ' He barked at the clattery voice, then came back. 'It's hit the sea four miles off

Flamborough. The one before. How the hell do they do it in the time?'

'There must be a complete insulation against the atmosphere,' I said. 'What other way is there?'

'Lost it,' Grey said.

There was just the night sky on the picture. The disc had been lost, gone ahead of us.

'They can't be rocket driven,' I said. 'You could never get that speed physically. Not with anything we know or are likely to know for a long time.'

'Radio. Light,' Grey said tersely. 'That's a way to speed. One-eighty thousand a second. Ride on that, or a part of that beam and you've got yourself a hot motor.'

He laughed and wiped his face.

Maggy came back. I hadn't noticed she'd gone.

'The chopper's overhead,' she said. 'And those damn weeds are screaming again. What are you going to do?'

'Who's going?' Grey bawled. 'Speak up!' Then he laughed again.

Nobody took any further notice.

'Nobody wants your airlift,' I told Harcourt. 'Signal him to stand off a bit. We may need him.'

Harcourt started talking offstage again, and several clattery voices seemed to be talking speaking with him.

'Pilot says it looks like a Gorgon's head outside your house,' he said to me. 'Some classical man, that.'

'He's clicked. It looks just like that. A land of waving snakes. They're going to pull this ruddy house down. Just tell him to stand off, he's shaking the building with his downdraught. It's weak already.'

'Wait.' He went off again.

'There's no more,' Grey said. 'That looked like the last.'

'Keep watching,' I said.

Potson gave another estimated plot of the last one's landing. A minute later Harcourt proved him right.

'In the mouth of the Forth,' he said. 'Got an air watch on the landing spots now, but still no trace. They seem to have sunk.'

'Being disc they probably went in edge on.'

'They still made a splash,' he said drily.

'They have some speed. Perhaps they depend on the braking force of water.'

'It's all guessing,' Grey said. 'We haven't materials that could stand that sort of treatment. Nor the people, either.'

'There's another!' Maggy said.

The same frightening impression of the terrific speed coming at us held us still. If these things hadn't been coming towards us we shouldn't have seen them at all.

But this one held. It blew up, a sudden awful blot.

I remember Grey yelling, 'Jesus!' and ducking. Perhaps everybody did. It was impossible to realize that this was a picture of something a long way out.

'That one's coming straight in,' Potson yelled. 'It's dead on the curve for here. Dead on!' His voice was higher than ever.

'Well, this is it,' Grey said. 'Give it a couple of minutes to arrive and the compression will blow us all to beggary. Get to the aircraft, Laura. Maggy. Go on out! Call him overhead!'

I called desperately. Harcourt reflected the alarm. The women ran through, Grey following them like a driver with whips. Potson stayed.

'Two-three minutes. There's a deceleration I can't graph, but it'll be about that.'

'Switch off!' Grey yelled back. 'The place is shaking to bits!'

It certainly was. The floors and doors were cracking and groaning as if the whole outside fabric of bricks was being twisted like a matchbox.

Potson started pulling switches. Dragging the phone cable with me I followed the evacuees through the rooms to the end one. The noise of the aircraft engine and the thrashing rotor were clear now the awful noise of the tramping machines was fading out. The building eased, as if willing to stand up a little longer.

Outside the window an ally rescue chair was coming down into view on the end of its cable, swinging and turning slowly. The noise of the helicopter was steady, but the rotor blades felt as if they thrashed the roof over our heads.

Maggy started to get out through the window on to the roof.

Potson suddenly rushed into the room,

crashed me aside with all his weight and grabbed the girl's arm.

'Don't! It's come — !'

That was all I heard him say and then the screaming began. It was like the others we had heard, not loud but penetrating. A giant sound that did not shriek.

We all looked up through that broken hole, up to the sky. The helicopter was silhouetted against the dull moonlit haze, a big black spider of a machine.

Then suddenly it whipped upwards and sideways, faster than any control could have moved it. It shot out of sight.

A frightful compression began in the air. Everyone clapped their hands over their ears to stop the sudden pain in the drums.

I saw the upper mist boil in a great circle like a giant splash in a pond, and the thing came down, alight, it seemed all over, as if enclosed in a case of brightly luminous glass.

Potson yelled and shoved the girl down against the wall. The far end of the room crumbled and started to fall outwards scattering bricks. The rafters sagged over our heads and the whole house shook and groaned with the great pressure in the air.

The disc came down into the middle of the weeds on the old car park. The great envelope of white fire suddenly stripped off it and lengthened as it sped upwards through the mist again, a small crack of thunder following its going.

The metallic blue disc, like a giant landmine, sat there immovable on the park, silent, still.

The aliens had landed.

5

The last bricks fell away, the sprawling ends of the rafters shivered and were still. The rest of the house still stood.

Maggy was crying on Potson's shoulder. Grey held Laura tightly as he stared out to the machine on the park I found my voice. My telephone was still mushing.

'Harcourt!' I remember whispering, as if the thing out there would hear. 'It's landed. Right outside. The helicopter was blown away. Haven't seen it since.'

'Pilot regained control,' he replied. 'But he said it was a squall. Unmanageable. Did the thing fire at it?'

'No. It was air compression.'

'Anybody hurt there?'

'No.'

'It is a machine, is it?'

'It's a disc. I'd say forty feet across, ten high. I don't see any windows. It looks smooth all round and on top.'

'I'm sending troops over. They'll stand off. You see what you think's best to do.'

'If I can think of anything. The weeds all round the thing have been burnt clean. About ten feet all round it.'

'No point in weed killer. I'll hold that . . . Anything happening?'

'I'll yell when.'

Curiosity had overcome primitive fears in all five of us then. We looked out through the broken wall and the whalebones of the roof. The disc stayed there immobile, sitting silent amongst the moaning weeds.

'Looked as if it comes in enveloped in a protective gas that insulates it against friction heat,' Grey said.

'Or it could be something that turns into gas and absorbs heat that way,' I said.

'Why doesn't it do anything?' Potson said, holding the girl tightly.

'So long as it doesn't I'm happy,' Laura said huskily.

Then it started to move. The top pushed up in a series of cylinders like a telescope, pushing up and up until the last section was quite thin. It went up and up into the night sky and stopped at a height of some two hundred feet.

Then a bowl stood up on its top, a metal pudding basin. It began to turn and to oscillate at the same time.

'A scanner,' Grey said.

'Spherical scan,' I said. 'Covering all planes but the one it stands on.'

The curious spin and wobble motion increased in speed until the whole thing looked like a translucent metal ball.

We all watched it up there spinning against the sky. I told Harcourt about it. He had a gaggle of experts there with him then — that is, if you can have an expert of something nobody knew anything about.

Then he came through.

'There's one off Flamborough. Plane spotted it. Sticking up like a drumstick. We can see it on the plane's TV right here — '

He broke off suddenly.

'What happened?' I said. Grey's head turned towards me, so did Laura's.

'Shot down by the look of it. Something flashed. The camera started swooping down, then blacked out.'

'So they're not friendly,' I said.

'That's a legitimate guess,' he said, and I heard him shout, 'Warn all planes to stand off. Five miles. No nearer.'

Our visitor still stood against the sky, bowl spinning, but did nothing else.

'Are there men inside?' Maggy said.

'Anything could be inside,' Grey said. 'Anything. Anything at all!'

'Stop the creep-talk,' Potson said. I saw him lick his lips.

Above the queer murmuring of the weeds we heard the roar of a plane in the distance making an approach on the airport. From our site the runway would be six miles south and running east west.

We saw a flash, a beam of light like a whip flick from the spinning pan upwards at an angle to the sky. There was an almost instant burst of orange fire down in the sky. It began to curve downward steeper and steeper, then suddenly fell in a shower of flame like a bursting rocket.

Grey wiped his face with his hand.

'So that's it. Anything flying — phizz! Better call that fact back to your friends.'

I found my voice and told Harcourt. He didn't answer me but barked to the others, giving orders.

'But they were just people — ordinary people!' Laura said desperately. 'Just burnt up — '

'This thing can't tell the difference between armed and unarmed aircraft,' Grey said. 'It's just against flying.'

The bowl went on spinning as if nothing had happened, grim, slender, silent, terrifying. A killing machine.

'Why doesn't it see us?' Maggy said. She shivered.

'Perhaps it isn't interested,' Grey said. 'Perhaps it knows how helpless we are.'

The floor suddenly gave a lurch. It felt as if it would go altogether, but with a rattle and creak it stopped again, sloping down to the broken wall.

The sudden shift to an understood risk seemed to shake everybody back to sanity. We backed up to the door but stayed far enough into the room to see out at what the thing was doing.

'This house is going to collapse sooner or later,' I said. 'We can't just stay. There must be a way that thing won't see us.'

'The weeds are all round,' Laura said. 'So what.'

I thought Potson would break in with the 'tried to eat me' reminiscence, but he stood there staring out at the machine.

'There's got to be a way,' Grey said. 'We can't stay with that thing there. Better to fight the weeds.'

'Too many,' Potson said. 'They'll get you down, trip you. They're thick as hell now.'

Maggy leant against the wall, her hair almost covering her face as she let her head fall miserably.

'It's no good,' she said. 'We'll never get out of here. I knew we never would. I knew if we waited we'd be sunk. We can't get out now.'

'Don't give in,' Potson said, a curious firmness in his voice. 'As Grey says, there has to be a way. We just have to think. Calculate. Collect the known factors.'

'The known factor is we've had it!' Maggy shouted raising her head. 'We'll never get out.'

'You're spoilt,' Potson said quietly. 'You think you can't have your own way any more. But you might do. If you don't give in.'

The transformation of the fat, apparently spineless lecturer was startling and invigorating. I could not see the real reason, that suddenly he felt stronger than the girl who had ruined him.

Also, I didn't remember then that the machines in the basement had stopped radiating.

'There's only the back of the house,' Laura said. 'And the gardens are wild with flowers and weeds, feet high. Worse than the car park. Also, they're climbing the walls at the back.'

'Right,' Grey said. 'Then the ground's out. Most of the back walls must be avoided. We can't climb with the weeds. We fly.'

'Very intelligent!' Maggy screamed.

'The flying trapeze act,' Grey went on, ignoring Maggy. 'Rope. Do we have any rope?'

Laura shook her head.

'Not even a clothes line,' she said.

'That's the trouble with sending everything to the laundry.'

Even in that broken room, with the monster outside and the crawling weeds trying to pull us down, Laura suddenly made the thing sound reasonable, homely. I wanted to laugh.

'A bridge,' Grey went on. 'A bridge to the back garden wall and the canal there. They can't be growing on the water.'

'Where's the canal?' I said.

'It runs along the back of the gardens. Just breaks cover for that distance, then goes back underground. Down to the river — ' He pointed east, ' — and up to one of the other canals, Regent's, Grand Central. I never bothered to find out.'

'Damn it!' I said. 'Does it still run through?'

'The water runs through, so I assume it does.'

'Then if we could reach it, there's our escape line!'

'Wingate, you are almost a genius,' he said quietly. 'But are we all in good condition to swim a mile or more? We have no boat in the house. It never seemed a worthwhile investment.'

'Never mind that,' Laura said. 'Get to the water first. Then see what we can do.'

'You're wasting your time!' Maggy said bitterly. 'How in hell do we get down there? We're nearly fifty feet up!'

'A bridge,' said Grey again. 'From up here down to the back garden wall.'

'It will be a hell of an angle,' Potson said.

'It will be easier to walk out and just let that thing lick the life out of you,' said Maggy. 'What's the good of playing boy scouts? We'll never get out of here. As soon as it sees we're here it'll lick us to nothing with that bloody thing on top.'

'Hope springs eternal in this human beast,' said Grey. 'We shall try and build a bridge.'

'What with?' Laura said.

'We've got the tools,' said Grey. He sounded very dry and sober.

'What else?'

'Floorboards,' I said. 'There's enough in the end room and all loose one end.'

'This is crazy, just crazy!' Maggy cried out. 'If it's going to be so easy, why did you just think of it? Why didn't we go that way before?'

'Because nobody wanted to go,' Grey reminded her sharply. 'Everybody wanted to stay and see what happened, if anything. By the time it did happen there wasn't any time to do anything.'

'We should have gone before,' she said. 'It's too late now. You know that!'

'Turn your back on the defeatist,' Grey said going out through the door. 'Potson, just calculate how much footage of bridge we shall want. Take a look out of the back landing.'

We all went through the rooms then, except Maggy. She stayed leaning back against the wall. On the landing Potson pulled the old shutters open as I had done before.

'Christ!' he said, and tried to shut them again.

The japonica burst in on us, waving, wandering, a mass of flowers and tendrils pawing the air like blind feelers. I went to Potson's aid. So did Grey. We shoved in panting silence while the flowers wailed softly and tried to force us back.

We got the shutters fixed again. The floor was covered in broken, writhing stems and leaves. A thin, half crushed line of pawing flowers and stalks reached in between the joint of the shutters. We got the iron bar across.

Laura just said, 'My God!' very softly. It sounded like a sigh of despair.

'Good-bye bridge,' Grey said. 'In the old days the hero could escape by going hand over hand along the telephone cable, but now they put them all underground — ' He shrugged. 'I'm going to get a drink.'

He lumbered away downstairs, walking heavily, a big, sagging body of a man, momentarily beaten.

'It's as good an idea as any,' Potson said, sounding very dry and harsh. 'Where's that stupid girl?'

He went back for her. Laura and I followed Grey downstairs.

'I think she's right,' Laura said in a half whisper. 'What chance do we stand? At any minute that thing could strike us dead. Maybe it hasn't seen us. That's all.'

Laura was wrong, but none of us had

the sense to see it then. To imagine that some obviously superior machinery like we had seen out there could not know we were in that house was just wishful thinking.

When we got to the study Grey was standing at the window looking up at the towering metal structure silhouetted against the night sky, the dizzy transparent ball spinning on top.

'It's a hell of a size,' he said huskily, and turned for his barrel.

The moon behind the high haze gave light enough for that room. Certainly no one was going to switch on a lamp.

He got a mug of beer, gave me one, and let Laura drink out of his. She stared out of the window. The weeds were a waving field almost as high as the sill now, which meant five or six feet.

'Well, it's been a novel experience,' Laura said, turning her back on it.

Potson came in carrying Grey's rough radio hookup and tripping on the telephone cable.

'This geyser's calling for you,' he said breathlessly.

I heard Harcourt chittering away like a distant parrot. I had completely forgotten that radio. It was a shock when I realized it meant that, at the back of my mind, I didn't think it mattered any more. I had forgotten it because it seemed no longer important. The bridge, the only hope, now gone made Harcourt feeble and unnecessary.

'What is it?' I said.

'These things have got a laser gun or something,' Harcourt said. 'It seems to lock on to the target then fire.'

'Aren't you getting any radio traces of what it is? Isn't there any interference, or signal, or something? They must be communicating with each other, mustn't they?'

'None of the monitors or tracking stations are getting a thing. Not even radar blips where they are. Planes can see them — from a long way off — but there are no echoes.'

'How many planes have you lost?' I said suddenly.

'Thirty-six,' he said, tonelessly. 'They all got too near, though some were over ten miles out. It's a long beam, this laser. All aircraft lost were inland or on the land side of the creatures. Spotters were Coastal Command over the sea. All flying has ceased. Civil stuff turned back to wherever they started from. We are now isolated by air.'

The flat recital sickened me. It sounded helpless, hopeless, defeated.

'What are the services going to do?' I said. 'Losing those planes is an act of war!'

'Which star do we declare war on?' he said, acidly. 'The service people have tried with planes to contact, and got burnt up. What do they do next? Burrow?'

'Submarines for the ones at sea.'

'They're going to try that. Nobody likes it. We can't tell yet what range these ray guns have. Could be way beyond torpedo range, even below water. They're going to try a shot at maximum range.'

He cut off then and talked offstage.

'Any good news?' said Grey ironically.

'Every war weapon has an Achilles' heel,' I said. 'The thing is, how do you find it when the instrument is alien and composed of materials strange to us?'

'By the fact of their burning up planes it doesn't look as if our materials are strange to *them*,' Grey said. 'They know what we've got that burns.'

Through the doorway I could see Maggy sitting on the stairs, arms on her knees, hands holding her bent head. She thought she could see the end. I thought I could, too. One whip of that laser beam and the whole lot would fall apart. What I couldn't understand is why it hadn't happened already.

'There's a certain logic in the air,' Potson said, staring up at the monster. 'It knows our radio systems because it re-sends our echoes. Then it must be monitoring your chat with the Ministry. Yet it hasn't jammed it.'

'What's logical?' Laura asked.

'It's listening so that it will know what we're going to do next. That's why it's leaving us alone. While we still contact the main brain at the Ministry, we're of value, so we don't die.'

'If that's the case,' Grey said, 'let's keep talking.'

'Richard?' The radio came on again. 'The torpedo. The thing exploded it miles off then got the sub as well, though on instruction it crash dived after releasing the weapon. Rocket missiles with homing heads have now been tried off the Forth. They were disintegrated miles off. We think now that scanner on top is an auto brain that operates the laser instantly anything is detected approaching it, above or below datum.'

The problem was whether to tell him Potson's theory of our survival. If I did, it might end our temporary security. And anyway, Harcourt couldn't tell me anything the things didn't themselves know.

In any case, he kept repeating, 'Are you all right?' A normal, human, daft question, because if we weren't we couldn't answer.

'We shall have to go on testing,' he said, and went off the air again.

By testing he meant use other methods, but I don't know what they were. If the things got anything that approached them, how in hell could anyone get at them? Send in a ghost battalion?

We had the answer with us. We had the means of escape, a way to victory in that room then and we couldn't see it. Yet even at that time we had all the information we needed.

'The weeds,' Potson kept saying. 'What makes them dance?'

He kept watching them and after some time he came up with something that was new.

'They're seeding and growing up in minutes,' he said. 'So presumably they must be dying as fast. And they are. If you look down now to where they broke up between the cobbles, you'll see it's thick with dead weeds.'

We all crowded to the window. Even in that dull light and the faint glowing of the weeds we could see he was right.

'Which means,' the fat man said, 'that this isn't a motorization of the inanimate at all. It's speeding up their lives so that they grow while we watch and that gives movement.'

'But they tried to eat you,' Laura said.

'They sucked on,' he said. 'But with that fantastic speed of growing up and dying it could give weird impressions that seem to be something they aren't.'

'One thing it does mean,' said Grey grimly, 'they must be using up oxygen at a hell of a rate, growing like that, opening and shutting by the minute instead of the day.'

'That explains why we behaved like a lot of drunks out there,' I said. 'I mistook it for complete panic.'

The idea that we were being spared for the time being had an enlivening effect for a short time. For an even shorter time we might have thought of the menacing tower as almost friendly, as a coward feels gratitude towards an enemy who stops on the point of the beat up, forgetting the choice remains with the beater.

'What metal is it?' Potson said. 'Looks like blue steel.'

'It's a very pretty tinge,' said Laura coldly and turned away from the window. 'I'm mad about it. Are these friends of yours going to do anything?'

'It's difficult to know what to do yet,' I said. 'They'll act when they get a clue to what's actually happening.'

'There was a lot of rain,' Grey said. 'Ten times more than we can account for. Is there no news at all from outside this country?'

I passed on the question. Harcourt repeated there was nothing yet. Then he got a call and changed his mind.

'UFO reported Berlin, but landed in East. No confirmation,' he said.

'One,' said Grey in disgust. 'There must be hundreds waiting out there. They'll be in.'

'Do you really think that thing's listening?' Laura said.

'I'd guess so,' Grey said.

'It's shuddering,' she said, shaking her head to get a horror thought out of it. 'I don't think it's human. I don't think it's animal. I think it's a bloody machine!'

'That's pretty obvious,' Grey said, wiping his face again.

'I mean, just a machine.'

'Oh!' Grey was suddenly angry and sarcastic. 'I suppose that's why our machines danced themselves to bits! It was a victory waltz. Up computers, kill the dreaded boss! You have nothing to lose but their brains — '

'Well?' She cut in sharply. 'What's impossible?'

'You are,' he said, and turned away to drink again.

'What did make them dance, then?' she persisted.

She was biting at him like a terrier.

'There must have been a crossed wire from the stuff upstairs!' he said. 'You know it's only in the experimental stage!'

'Don't shout,' she said. 'I always know you're not sure of yourself when you shout.'

He stamped out into the hall, clutching his mug to his chest, glaring ahead.

'He'll never discuss anything,' she said, turning to me. 'That's why we've had all these troubles with the councils and the Ministries. He just bawls them out. Not that they don't deserve it, but it just stops you getting anywhere.'

'Don't stir him up,' I said. 'We need his brain working, not his emotion.'

'Thanks,' she said turning cold.

'Well, it's right, isn't it?'

She turned away. Potson looked back

from the window.

'If the weeds are growing at that speed, are we?' he said.

It jolted me sick. I felt ill.

'How can we?'

'We wouldn't notice for a few hours,' he said. 'Relative to the life of a weed. You understand me?'

'Yes. But we'd feel it,' I said. 'We'd be moving quicker.'

'No. We haven't the muscular means to move that quick. It's more likely to make you feel heavy. It's only the decay that's speeding up.'

'Oh, shut up!' I shouted at him.

But he was intense.

'You could destroy a world in a few weeks that way. Race it to death. Leave the throttle wide open. Do you realize that?'

'You want to cool off.'

'Are you frightened of my thinking?' He laughed, but it was a sore sound. 'How do you know I'm not right? The aircraft. They appear to explode. But suppose this ray speeds up the decay of its metals — like that screaming bit of metal in the cabinet — the plane would burst as if something had hit it. It's not a laser ray. It's a ray that speeds up decay so that the atomic structure changes too quickly. That's what is is. My calculations are borne out by everything that's happened — '

'Talk to this man,' I said, giving him the phone.

The line was chattering with police calls now. Grey had chimed in on a spare police frequency, but it was beginning to be used.

'Hang on,' I said, snatching it back. 'Just for a minute.'

I listened to the ghost calls coming through.

'The damn front gardens have started dancing all down Ebury Walk,' a policeman reported. 'Never seen anything like it. Come alive, flowers, bushes and those plane trees down the pavements — all waving about, dancing about — Some women have started to scream and run. Better have a couple of ambulances to start with. But what do we do next?'

This was representative of several other

calls coming through, all jumbled, police-men not waiting their turn to come in but yelling all at once.

'Keep them calm, keep them calm,' I heard the station sergeant's voice talking like a parrot, not understanding the order he was giving.

'Tell them what?' one officer shouted louder than the others.

'Tell them anything. Keep them calm.'

A sharper voice cut in then.

'Get off this frequency.'

Voice by voice the line cleared to mush. Harcourt came on again.

'This disturbance is spreading pretty widely,' he said. 'The weed animation. Can you see anything happening?'

'Nothing. Wait. I'll give you a man with an idea. Anything might help.'

So Potson went on the line and talked. After a while he handed the phone back but Harcourt had cleared. I laid it on the table.

'He's putting the idea before his advisers,' Potson said, his face running with sweat so that it dripped on to his fat chest and ran down his belly. He believed his theory if anybody did. He was boiling with it. 'I'm sure it's the one.'

'Yes, but — ' I just didn't go on because I couldn't think of anything to refute his nightmare.

'It links up everything,' he went on, intensely. 'The walking weeds, the machines — Remember the machines! Like the bit of rocket in that cabinet, writhing, worming about, screaming with its inner changes. The same with the machines, their inside wriggling like a box of worms trying to get out, all the wires and the copper circuits, the transistors and condensers racing their hearts out, burning so hot they can't stop when the life blood is switched off. Because the electricity that's making them writhe is generated by their own atomic decay.'

'You sound as if you enjoy it!' I said.

'I can be right, you know,' he said, his voice hissing down to a whisper.

'Yes,' I said. 'I think you could be. And if you are, how the hell can you combat such a weapon? It means ultimate destruction within a short time. Those weeds out there can't go on at that pace.'

'They'll grow stunted, then more stunted and finally burn up because they can't absorb oxygen enough to feed such a pace of life. And when they've used the oxygen, we will die. We don't have to grow old in a few weeks. We'll die without oxygen much, much sooner than that.'

We had almost forgotten Laura. She was sitting at the end of the table, making circles on the cloth with her fingertip and staring down at it. Grey was in the doorway, staring at Potson.

'Where did you get this idea?' Grey said.

Potson turned to him and shrugged.

'How can you tell when an idea really starts, or where? The baby begins with the ape of a million years ago. I could have read something, somewhere, about decay and death being a natural chemical process and not a senseless rotting away. Who said that the pear that rots must have power within to do it? They're using the power within that all life on earth has already planted in it. Stimulating it. Creating chemical reaction.'

'You say that metal is a form of life?' I said.

'What else is it? It could have no form without the living molecules. Metal could not fatigue were it not alive. It could not wear out or break, take cold or hot.'

'That's carrying a thought too far,' I said shortly.

'Why did the end of the house collapse?' He asked. 'Why was the house shivering long before the machines danced?'

'The weeds,' I said.

I saw Laura shake her head at her endlessly circling finger. She did not look up, and the gesture made me think I must be wrong.

'It wasn't outside,' Potson said. 'It was inside. You could feel that with all your nerves.'

Grey came to the table and stopped there rubbing his bristly face. Nobody noticed Maggy leaning against the door-post, almost hanging on to it for support.

'Look at him?' She pointed at Potson. 'Forty-six pounds in a week! Look at father. Like a balloon to what he was.

Look at me! Fifteen pounds in four days. And we didn't eat! Only mother made us, and she didn't come unless she had to. He must be right. Jack must be right. It isn't fat we're putting on, it's age!'

'Since we noticed the heat, the humming,' Grey said and sat down by Laura. 'It's been since then.'

'If they managed to cause this speed-up from out in space, why come in now?' I said. 'They could have waited. Speeded it up from out there.'

'It could have been they didn't know it was already working,' Grey said.

'He told them,' Laura said. She did not look at him but just nodded her head that way.

'You're crazy,' Grey said.

'He told them!' she repeated. 'That was why he signalled all the time. Morning, noon and night he was calling them.'

'They never answered!' He was getting wild again.

'You got signals,' Maggy said, puzzled.

'They weren't answers. I never knew what the hell they were. It's hard to tell, out there in the depths. You could be

168

fooled by a good many things including stars exploding.'

'You weren't fooled. You knew.' Still Laura kept watching her circling finger.

'Are you accusing me of bringing these bloody things here?'

For a moment I thought he might hit her, his wild Irish temper was so easily roughed up. But an odd thought occurred and Laura put it into words.

'Why are you so wild if you didn't?' she said. 'Is your conscience hackling for nothing? That's not like you.'

'How the hell could I contact these goons? We can't talk!'

'You know — ' she began.

'My God, look!' Potson shouted. 'Armoured hovercars. Over in the far corner there! Look!'

We jumped up and swarmed at the window. Coming down the old derelict street right across the car park was a force of five hovercars, creeping along towards the monster in the middle of the desolation.

Some fool Army commander had decided to try his luck.

6

We watched the creeping line of vehicles coming down the narrow street. Then Maggy called out.

'There's more down there!'

She pointed to the left. Putting our faces close to the panes we saw a further force creeping along, coming up on the car park from our left. They were still protected by ruined buildings.

When we saw them, we looked to our right. More of them showed coming round behind the broken buildings at the end of the street.

It was an attempt at encirclement. I looked up at the radar bowl spinning on top of the tower. It seemed to be doing nothing.

One of the cars came within sight — just. We saw his blinding beam from the laser gun shoot up towards the monster, but too late. The bright, thin whip from the high bowl flashed down. It seemed like a wand moved under an arc lamp, flicking on and off at terrific speed. It whipped the leading car and there was sudden fire and a burst of greenish flame shot upwards. The wand swept out to the force on our left.

There again the green burst flared into the night and we heard a rumbling, but no explosion.

The whiplash then swept right up into the sky over our heads and swept down to the force on our right. This time there were three bursts of green light and the rumble was loud and shook the house as bombs would.

The whip flashed up and then off and the bowl stayed spinning up against the sky.

Seven of the cars which had tried to break out and strike the monster were just sulphuric bowls of green glowing smoke. We saw some of the others retreat back down the streets and out of sight.

As I describe it, it seems that the whole thing was very slow, even leisurely. In fact, the whole action took no more than a few seconds.

The women turned away from the window.

'Well, that's that,' Grey said. 'There's no better weapon in our gun rooms than the laser cars. And there they are, chemically realigned.'

I went back to the phone and told Harcourt.

'We got TV pictures from the rearmost cars,' he said dully. 'There's a slow motion print coming up now on the tape. Hold it. Infra red, this one . . . '

There was a long pause. It seemed they were re-running the tape. Grey gave us cigarettes.

'We've re-taped on the slow motion and got it slower still,' Harcourt said. 'It looks as if the laser beams were bounced back off the spinner to the cars. The science boys are just trying to work out if that's possible.'

I put the phone down and told the others.

'This is adding up,' said Grey. 'They've got auto resenders to fox our radar. Now they have a bouncer for laser. The similarity between the two systems is very considerable. There is one big common factor. The speed of 180,000 miles a second, light and radio being the same.'

'What do you begin to see?' Potson said, sweating again.

'These are radio people,' Grey said. 'They're using radio for everything. For deception, defence, attack — the lot. It's radio. Highly adapted, but it's recognizable radio.'

'You still say you didn't bring these bastards?' Laura burst out. 'You're a liar. Didn't you see what happened out there? Didn't you see it?'

'What do you mean?' he shouted back. 'Of course I saw it! The attack failed!'

'There were cars there — ' she pointed to the left of the window, then swung her hand across it and pointed to the right, 'and more there. The obvious way for that thing to fire was straight across from one lot to the other.'

She swung her hand back and forth horizontally.

'But it didn't do that. It swung right up and over this house then down on to the cars over there. It swung right up and over! It knows we're in here! It knows *you're* in here. And you're their friend, Car! That's why it went over our heads. That's why!'

She was on the point of tears and sat down suddenly at the table again and let her face drop into her hands.

'Well, what's the matter with that?' Grey said. 'You ought to be bloody glad you're not dead!'

Maggy was staring at her father from the doorway.

'Did you arrange with them?' she said huskily.

'Of course I didn't! How could I? I don't know their language.'

'If their language is radio,' said Potson, 'that's yours too. It isn't necessary to talk to communicate. Birds don't. Dogs don't. But they can communicate over great distances. Their messages are sent, received and understood without talk or sound. It's possible that's what you've been doing with these people and you didn't realize it.

'Obviously they've been listening and monitoring our crude radio signals for years as we might listen to crickets in a hedge. Then suddenly, out of this lot, a solitary, sophisticated signal — from you. They lock on. They believe they've found one of themselves on this planet. One brought in with the contamination of that rocket. Perhaps a sperm. Anything that could have incubated and grown. One of them, Grey.'

He wiped his sweating face with his hand, then rubbed it on his equally wet belly. Grey didn't say anything for a long time.

'It's possible,' he said at last. 'But accidental if it is possible. A side effect, say. A side effect of using way out frequencies. Yes, could be.'

'If it is true, why don't they come out and over here?' Maggy said quickly. 'Why don't they contact you?'

'What do you think they are — hams from outer space? Drop in for tea any time. All welcome.' He went on. Nobody listened.

Maggy clicked on a transistor radio, and suddenly we were not so far from the outside world, but it did not sound too good a world to be back in.

' . . . the public are warned not to approach any strange object but to report the matter to the police at once. The seafronts of the following towns are to be evacuated forthwith. The police will direct you . . .

'Warning to shipping. The following sea areas are now declared dangerous to all shipping . . . '

'At least they're doing something,' Laura said. 'They might have tried to keep it quiet and deal with it behind the scenes.'

'This one's too scary,' I said.

I thought of those seafront towns and the people, suddenly thrown into panic by the dancing weeds, and the warning to get out. I thought of them running, of the cars jamming up, of the whole system throttling itself with fear. And off the shore the spinning bowl striking up from the sea, watching, doing nothing while the defenders were running away . . .

There was a long list of places and warnings, and notices of arrangements being made, some of them I recognized as being parts of the old Civil Defence set-ups designed to save some from nuclear attack.

Maggy got screwed up and snapped the set off. I think we were all glad.

'War,' Potson said, dully.

'But they don't attack until you approach them,' Grey said. 'It seems so far purely defensive.'

'Which is a great comfort,' Laura said sourly. 'But if you're right, can't we get out somehow and go? We wouldn't go towards that damned thing. So you say it would let us go without doing anything. Besides, it wouldn't kill *you*.'

'We've already discussed this getting out,' I said. 'If Potson's right about the weeds and what makes them move, we could wade through them with a billhook, a scythe or something. But it infers the invader won't do anything. I wouldn't risk it's good offices.'

We watched from the window, the three men. Nothing happened outside. Once there was a crash and scattering of bricks from upstairs, crashing down amongst the weeds on the pavement.

I ran upstairs, with Grey behind me, but it was more of the end room falling away. The weeds were showing in the ragged opening, waving against the cold, glowing blue of the thing on the car park.

'It'll all go, gradually, the whole house,' he said, turning back.

We went into the radar room. There was a single green pilot light still on there. He stopped and looked around him.

'Pity, all this work,' he said, then shrugged. 'I have a two-way guilt about it. That I did it and brought these things. That I can't save it now.'

'You cut less out of the fabric of this house than the others. It has a bit longer chance.'

He leaned against the wall.

'Do you really think I did it? Side effect, dead ahead effect? Any way at all through this apparatus?'

'It's too much of a coincidence that the centre pin landed here. From the positions of these things, there is a kind of radial spoke layout centring on this one outside. So this is the hub for whatever will happen. You had the only machinery that could watch them. They didn't jam yours out or re-send as they did the others. So it really does seem that you did it.'

'Ah! It would have happened anyway, somewhere, someday. Invasion on this scale isn't a probe. We have a dozen here and another hundred or two standing off out there, waiting to come in. Do you agree with that?'

'Yes. I think it's designed to land these things by darkness. So they wait out there until the shadow blots the land and then go in. So it should be the States next, then on round, China, India, Africa and so complete the ring.'

'But why?' he said, heavily. 'Have you really thought why? They come here. They're known now. Every country in the world has now been alerted. You know that. Yet they sit there doing nothing. They sit there, like repellent flypaper, just driving off the human fly, but doing nothing. They're not building anything, unloading anything. They just sit there.'

'But they've stopped all flying. That's a big help in an invasion.'

'Why don't they do something, something positive? Stopping flying is the negative result of sitting there as flypapers. They have an automatic, lock-on, homing device for burning up things that come near. But action? None!

None whatever. Nothing has moved in that thing but the saucepan spinning on top. What's it waiting for?'

'If Potson's right and you did contact this lot,' I said, 'can't you try and find out more?'

'It means using this ruddy outfit, and you know what happens downstairs.'

'Can't we chain them down? Tip 'em over or something so they can't dance?'

His answer came from the end room. There was a creak, a crash and thudding of bricks falling. He just shrugged.

'Can't risk the house falling before it's got to,' he said. 'As it is it could last a few hours yet. With the machines hopping, I wouldn't give it twenty minutes.'

'Why didn't they hop all the time you've been using this frequency?'

'I can't quite work that out, but they were overheating, behaving abnormally all the time. They were giving off some kind of radiation. You felt it yourself. I can only guess the overheating went too far after a long period of insemination, and the atomic overheating erupted. What a splendid lot of words. Pity we don't know if they mean anything.'

I gave him a cigarette and took one myself.

'Can't you work back to where you started on this radar circuit?'

'I can do that. It would take time and a lot of Potson's figurative brain. Why?'

'It's possible that in one of the steps you took there is the explanation to this side effect. What seems important is that it's the same as they're using. You made the machines dance and they did the weeds, it seems. But its the same effect. I'm sure of that.'

'You think that thing is going to sit there doing nothing long enough to give us time?'

'I think Laura's right. They won't touch you.'

'Suppose we find this link? What can we do with it?'

'It might make it possible to talk.'

'With what words, Wingate?'

'Just find the link first. Remember what Potson said about the dogs and birds. There is a way. Somebody has to find it sometime. Try now.'

He went on smoking, thinking hard.

Potson called out from below and I went out to the landing.

'Your Ministry came on again,' he said. 'It's a radio network. This weed dance is now reported countrywide, fields, pastures, bushes, forests — the lot. All moving. There's a king size panic breaking out all over the place. Police are trying to deal with it. He's gone off again. Said to tell you.'

Grey was standing in the doorway watching me. I turned back to him.

'Try,' I said. 'What with weeds and panic excitement oxygen must be getting rare in some places.'

'It won't notice yet,' he said and turned back. 'Send Laura up. She took a lot of notes originally. She might remember.'

I went down and told Laura.

'The beginning?' she said. 'It was years

ago! In fact, I don't remember an actual beginning. He's been playing about with this kind of thing for years. It's developments more than beginnings.'

She was hesitant, doubtful, but she went up, hauling heavily on the handrail, head bent, trying to remember.

It was one of those situations where an outsider might remember, whereas the inventor himself, having skated over it with his eyes on a further star, might not. It was a hope at that time, when nobody knew anything.

Maggy was sitting on the stairs. I had to squeeze by. She didn't seem to notice I was there. Potson was in the study.

'He said if anything happens, to ring back. He won't call again. Too busy. Up to you from this end.'

'Do you know what's been tried?'

'The defence services are all in confab, but I don't know what they've got to talk about constructively. I think the solution to this has got to be unarmed.' He looked out of the window again. 'If there is to be a solution. We don't have to escape all the time.'

Maggy heard him. She gasped, and then suddenly I saw her run past the open door. Potson spun round, and then, with surprising speed for his fatness, he tore out into the hall.

'Mag! Don't be a fool!' He roared out.

I heard the door rattle open as I got into the hall. She was out before he could reach her, plunging down the steps to the waving, dying weeds. They had thinned out with death, but the living still stood four or five feet high.

She rushed into them striking out to push them aside, like a nightmare swimmer in a sea of weeds. Potson hesitated, his memory of the terror before holding him back. But as I got to the step he went on down. She was getting through them then, fighting her way from sheer panic.

She had let go. This was the reaction to never having been stalled or opposed. This was the madness we might have guessed would happen.

He shouted as he started after her, wading in, beating the stuff back like a machete man in the jungle. But he was in no panic, he wouldn't make her speed.

I went after them. They were beating a path through that the weeds were taking some seconds to fill again. But they were coming up from the ground as well, glowing redly in the night.

She went ahead, directly for the blue steel thing towering into the hazy moonlit sky. The green smoke still rising lazily from the burnt out hovercars, the dull purple red glow of the struggling weeds, and the blue steel thing rising up into the smoky, silver sky, all made a weird panorama of unearthly colours. Potson's naked, sweating back was shining copper, the girl's yellow hair thick like tow as it shook and flowed with her desperate flight.

'Maggy, come back, come back!' He kept on panting out the words and the effort, in the thin air, made him slower still.

I heard her sobbing as she fought on, and then suddenly she reached the cleared ring round the alien tower. She ran like mad then, straight for it. Potson called out, but she went on.

He broke free and I was close behind him then.

She must have been a half dozen yards from the base of the tower when a slit appeared in its side and widened. A door slid open and we could see a greenish light within.

'My God! Something's coming out!' Potson shouted.

We both stopped. The hysterical Maggy ran on, into the door and inside. The door stayed open. There was no sound from the tower. Maggy's panting and wild sobs had gone. There was only the murmuring of weeds outside.

We stood staring and Potson began to breathe again, hard, quick. Then once more courage overcame his fears and he started to run towards the open doorway.

This time I called to stop him as he had tried to stop the girl. He just ran on. Then, so did I.

What made me do it, I had no idea. It wasn't any emotion of mine that motivated my going, but a sudden unmanageable urge to go. I felt I must go, had to go, as if something pulled me towards that door.

Potson ran in. I did not see what happened to him or to Maggy. They had been swallowed into silence within the structure.

I went on and into the doorway. A frightening silence enveloped me. I turned and saw the door slide shut. The inside was as smooth as the outside had been, no mark of where the door was.

The place I stood in was a narrow passage. On either side there were metal cabinets, plain blue metal like the outside, the greenish light making it almost black. The floor was a chequered design, plastic, stone, metal, any guess was good then.

I went on. At the end there were four more passages, radiating from a central pivot like a five pointed star.

Potson stood there, staring upward. Maggy was in another passage, just standing there, looking back at us.

Upwards I saw there was no ceiling to this central spot but the cylinder walls ran up and up to a terrifying height until they seemed to meet in a vast distance above.

'There's nobody here!' Maggy whispered, holding her hair back from her huge eyes. 'Nobody in here at all!'

Potson looked down from staring at the vast height, and swayed and fell against a cabinet, dizzy from his sight travel up that tower.

'Why did you run?' he said hoarsely.

'I had to,' she said. 'I had to!'

We stood there, afraid in the silence. I made my voice work against the dryness of my throat.

'It's recognizable engineering,' I said. 'There must be a kind of man animal behind it somewhere.'

'Not here,' Potson said. He seemed to have stopped sweating. It was cold and still in that place.

'Something made me come,' she said, wondering. 'It called, perhaps.'

'Or perhaps you just lost your head,' Potson said.

'But it opened for me. The door opened for me!'

'It stayed open for the three of us,' I said. 'Yet there's nobody in here. Laura was right. There is nothing inside. It's a machine. Just a machine.'

'Why did the door open, then? Do you mean they all do this? That the others can be approached?' Maggy said.

'You know they can't,' I said. 'Approachers get wiped out. We must be friends of your father's. I don't know why the bowl didn't flash us dead otherwise.'

'A machine can't differentiate like that,' Potson said.

'But it did. So it must be operated from somewhere else.'

'Grey's frequency,' said Potson suddenly. 'I wonder? We've all been impregnated with those frequency rays. Are we radiating? If we are, the machine could differentiate!'

'But why bring us in?' she said, looking round. 'Why? Nothing's happening.'

'If the opening was automatic, like a dog on a scent, nothing has to happen,' I said.

There was no echo in that place. Our voices were killed as soon as we had spoken.

'This is a service gallery,' Potson said. 'Mechanic's Alley. But it operates as an unmanned aircraft. It seems to bear out what we thought; it is a deliberate, mechanical means of running the world out quick so as to make way for somebody else to come in.'

'Won't everything be destroyed, going on like this?' Maggy said.

'It will mean a chemical rearrangement,' I said. 'Perhaps they don't need the same organisation as we do. If the earth's surface turned into putrefying gas, how do we know that isn't what they're used to living in?'

'You make me sick!' she shouted suddenly.

'Oh shut up,' Potson said, and turned away. 'I'm going to look down all these corridors and see if there's anything different. There must be machinery up in those telescope cylinders to push them up, so there must be a way up from this floor.'

His mathematical mind was working again, as if emotion with him, was but an occasional disturbance he could turn his back on.

The girl went after him, I thought, to

row with him but there was no word as they walked away. I explored another corridor and found nothing but the blank end, which might have had another door in it, but as they did not seem to have cracks all round their doors, I didn't know.

Potson called out. I went back into the centre of the wheel and saw him and Maggy at the end of another passage.

When I got there he was pointing to a metal staircase that rose up from beyond the last of the cabinets. The stairs went up to a height of about ten feet and then just ended nowhere.

'What's the good of that?' I asked. 'It just reaches the ceiling when the whole thing is closed up.'

'How are we going to get out of here?' Maggy said.

'I've been looking,' I said. 'There isn't a switch or a knob or a keyhole or anything. Not a lever or a wheel. The whole thing is automatic. There's no provision for anything to be operated at all.'

'Perhaps they don't have any hands,' she said, and shivered.

Potson stood there, frowning at the chequered floor.

'I don't sense any attempt to communicate,' he said. 'Yet outside two or three times I felt there was a try.'

'I did, too,' Maggy said. 'I felt it strong. It isn't here now. I feel just silly.'

'Lack of oxygen,' I said. 'That could be dulling our senses.'

'Is there any ventilation in here?' Potson said suddenly. 'There's air. How did that get here? This thing came down in a bag of hot gas.'

'It could have opened when the bowl went up on top. The door opened and there was no bang.'

We were talking like fools. The air we had in that metal box had all been supplied from out over the weeds. There couldn't have been any point in aerating an automat where every cabinet was sealed without joints, and even the metal hull had no cracks.

'What we're in is just an electronic lethal weapon,' Maggy said. 'I hadn't thought of it like that till now.'

Then she leaned back against what we

thought were stairs. The floor began to rise. It was a sudden silent swoosh of movement which pinned our feet to the floor, thrust our bowels down inside us, stole the thin air from our mouths.

It went on hundreds of feet up it seemed until the down-thrust let our bodies catch up and ease a little.

'Where in hell?' Potson said.

We were in space, standing there with stars millions of miles under our feet. Maggy screamed and fell against the fat man. He clasped her. I shut my eyes and prayed or cursed, I don't remember.

Then I opened my eyes and heard the familiar screaming, undulating sound, but deep, almost soothing.

Space was all round me, I was just there in the blue vastness as if I could reach out and touch stars floating past in the void.

But then, beyond the space vision, I saw a vast panorama of shore and sea and cliff and islands. It was as if the scene was painted on celluloid beyond a celluloid space, but both scenes were three dimensional. And there were figures, some kind of numbers done in braille, drifting fast across the vast nothing at my feet. From each character thin gold radial lines radiated, like compass points, or sight bearings on an ancient sea chart.

Then I saw another radial system of lines, but almost edge on, like looking sideways at a golden spider's web.

From these moving, interweaving bearing lines one could get an instant calculation of distance, depth, time.

We were in the topmost piece of the monster. The scenes glowing all round us, globelike, were the echoes coming in from the bowl above our heads. It was a human, or animal, check point.

'Geometry,' I heard Potson say. 'Splendid geometry!'

He was holding Maggy still but staring right through me as if to some gorgeous vision miles past my back.

I saw her try to push him off but his strength was more than she thought. He did not seem to notice the small, spasmodic effort.

'You recognize it?' I said.

'It must be universal,' he said. 'Geometry is the science of the stars, depthless, always predictable.'

'You're drunk!' she said.

'It's like the way we do it?' I said. 'I did geometry, but have forgotten such a lot.'

'This is a perfect version,' he said, staring round him. 'One could measure anything here and never make an error.'

Until he started speaking I didn't realize that the moving webs of the rings and radials were not only interlinked, but metering on the star scene and the land scene that was set beyond it.

'You mean that its recognizable as part of a system that we use?' I persisted.

'Oh yes. Yes, this is perfect. This is magnificent, but so simple. You see a vernier on every curve, with the intersections moving against the main graph. You could project the face of the Earth in a minute with this and never draw a bloody line! Never write a symbol, never make a point. In depth —'

'The pictures seem to be one on top of the other,' I said.

'Pictures!' He laughed suddenly. 'This

is the global scene — from within. This is space from a single point, the back picture I guess is being received from the others round the coast —'

'Lethal!' the girl hissed. 'It's a bomb. What's the difference? Magnificent! You must be mad! How do we get down? How do we get out?'

This time she shoved him away from her and then, to stop herself falling into nothing she grabbed the ladder behind her.

Obediently, we started to go down again. She gave a short scream and jumped away. The ladder stopped and so did we, still standing with our feet in outer space, but now there was a further picture beyond the stars.

For a moment I couldn't make it out, then I saw the City surrounding us, buildings and towers splayed out from the centre like rays of a sunburst.

'Why a ladder that makes a ladder unnecessary?' Potson said.

As I looked up at him I saw a piece of the land pictures through a square formed by the rungs. The picture broke into prismatic segments, colour bands running vertically and changing as I moved my head to see a different part of the headland.

I bent slightly to look through another of the squares. Again there was a prismatic superimposition on the head-land, but this time the colour formation was different.

'Geological,' I said. 'It gives the actual strata forming the land. Look. Through this one, I seem to remember that analysis is for copper. The one above I don't know, but its different.'

'So these things are actually surveying,' Potson said, eagerly. 'Then why the antagonism? Or is that accidental, a side effect of the survey beams?'

The girl turned and touched the ladder. We went down through the deep cylinder and came to the floor again.

'How do we get out?' she said, breathless.

'You got in,' Potson said, in a curious tone. 'You led us in. That's why you came. To get us in. That always is your amusement. To trap.'

I saw then that he was reeling and fell with his back against one of the cabinets. He was drunk with oxygen lack.

'I didn't expect this!' Maggy said. 'I thought there would be somebody —I didn't know it would be like this!'

I remember being only mildly surprised and not even angry that she had done the same thing to us as she had done to Potson. That sitting moodily on the stairs had been a time of working herself into a state where she could do it. No one, nothing had called from the tower. The compulsion had been in its radiation activity, I'd thought. But she knew the call from something else.

'You meant to do this, then?' I said. 'Since when?'

'They wanted to know,' she said, savagely sulky, apparently less affected by the thin air than we were.

'You mean that up there we were spectrum analysed by that ladder thing just as we were seeing the analysis of the headland?'

'They want to know,' she repeated.

'But how did they tell you?' I said, and

got her by the arm. 'How did they tell you, Maggy?'

She said nothing. I couldn't even see her face for the hair overhanging her downturned face.

'Did they speak somehow?'

'They told me,' she said.

'But how? How?'

'She imagines. She's crazy with it, like her father,' Potson said. 'You don't know what it was like in that house. The machines got you so you really wanted these things to come. I know. I began to feel it myself. So when you came I hated you for a spy. That's what they thought of you too, she and Grey. A spy. Working against them. Against me. You don't know how this thing affects you after a time. It gets in you, like a damned worm, wriggling about in your bowels, trying to make you love it.'

'You're drunk,' I said. 'But go on. What made you feel like that?'

'Machines. I don't know. Machines. Computers. They make errors, those things. Like Grey says, one kick wrong somewhere and the cube root of thirty million comes out as seven. They were burning up all the time. They couldn't cope. They got hot.'

He just leaned against the cabinet and stayed with his mouth open, trying to get more air in it. It might have been the extra weight he had put on to what must have been a heavyweight before.

'They asked me,' Maggy said. 'I thought there would be somebody here. Somebody.'

She talked like a child. I suppose I was vague, too, but didn't realize it. It seems clear now, but it was damned confusing then because everything seemed so easy, the more I lost control of myself.

'Who told you?' I said.

'They told me.'

'But how did they? Did you use the translator? The thinkbox? That one your father doesn't use any more?'

'It burnt out!' Suddenly she was angry, with a last wriggle of emotion before the don't-care set in again.

'You didn't say it burnt out. You said he wouldn't use it because it picked up your thinks too.' I knew I should have said thoughts, but I was incapable of changing from what I remembered she had said.

'We must get out of here,' Potson said, making an effort. 'I'm going to die.' There was no emotion about the words, just a plain statement.

Sometimes when it seems it's no good holding on any more against odds, an idea comes. It came then. As I felt the pleasant softening of my brain the rainbow colours of the tower top seemed to crowd in on my thoughts, pushing, jostling, the rainbow analyses of metals and stones, of woods and people's bodies and thoughts —

And then it hit me and shook me wide awake.

'Not radio!' I shouted to force myself to act against the drugged feeling. 'It's light. Light. Light!'

I started to walk to where we had got in. I remembered hitting the cabinets with my shoulders on both sides, and the girl panting somewhere behind me. I turned right round once and saw fat Potson crawling along on his hands and knees, panting like a tired dog.

We came to the rounded metal wall and I leant against it, trying to remember what I had meant to do. I couldn't. Potson came up and stopped, his head hanging down.

'Go on! Go on!' the girl said.

'I can't — remember.' I said that as I struggled to find the idea that had come and gone.

'You said light, light,' she said, banging my shoulder with her fist in time with the repetition. 'Light, light, light, light, light!'

When it came back I didn't believe it could have been what I'd thought.

I looked at the blank wall. She went on hitting me, but it didn't seem to hurt for she had no strength.

I fumbled for my trousers pocket but couldn't find the slot. My hand kept slipping down my side and I started to laugh, but it made me gasp for breath and I had to double up to get it back.

When I found my pocket once again I'd forgotten what I wanted. I brought out the little torch, and then searched for something else in there, money, keys and tried to recall what I must have.

'Light, for God's sake, you said light!' she said, despairingly.

The torch was lying in my hand. I looked at it again and the meaning came through the rainbow clouds in my brain.

The little light shone on the metal as I pressed the button. The wall dissolved, it seemed and I fell out on to the rough ground.

As I rolled I saw Potson, on his feet now, holding the edge of the opening for support. Then he threw himself out and went reeling past me towards the weeds.

It was an effort to get to my feet and when I did I couldn't balance and went headfirst into the girl. We fell over together and I heard shouting from somewhere.

When I got to my knees the opening had gone and only the plain blue metal stayed. I hauled the girl up, but she hung by an arm, scrabbling at the ground.

'I can't,' she kept gasping the words.

Again I lost my breath and let her go, having to double up. Somebody grabbed my hand and pulled me. I nearly went over again but came up against a strong, soft body that resisted my overbalance.

In the rainbow mists around me I saw Grey's shape picking up Maggy. Then we were struggling and stumbling through the waving weeds, tripping, but never quite falling because of the woman's calm strength.

I fell on the house steps but didn't feel anything. Somebody went by. The woman was pulling me.

'Get him in quick! Give me his hand!'

I was dragged up the steps, tearing the skin of my shins but never felt a thing of it. Once on the hall floor the door was slammed.

'Leave him there.' I recognized Grey's voice, only it seemed to be coming from beyond the edge of life.

7

Recovery was swift in the still normal air of the closed house.

'It's light, light is the answer,' I was saying this when my mind clicked straight. 'Not radio. Light. What did you use light for?'

'Laser's in the scanners,' Grey said. 'It's giving a frequency multiplication of the radio beams.'

'What happened to the translator, the thought translator?'

'It burst.'

Then I saw the girl's head move quickly, but she went still again without having met Grey's eye.

'They won't tell you,' Laura said quickly. 'It's a conspiracy. There always has been a conspiracy between the two of them. They won't tell you what happened.'

'Brainwashed,' Potson said. 'That's what the machines did to them when they plugged that thinker in. It read thoughts all right, but it took them out of you and put other ones back. That was what was wrong with the whole bloody thing. It got in your head all right and kicked everything out that was yours it didn't want. I had some of it. But I think in figures. That's my life, my mind. Figures. No political significance in figures. Why get rid of numbers? Nothing dangerous there. Might be useful when the invasion comes. So they didn't drive much out of me. They just left me frightened to death they would come back in one day and change their minds.'

'Into the house?' I said.

'Into my mind,' he said. 'Ask Grey what happened to that evil box. Ask him. See if he really can remember now that he's frightened.'

'It burst,' Grey said.

'It had to go,' Maggy said, altering the theme of the lie. 'It read what people were thinking. It was horrible.'

'What did happen to it?' I asked, and looked at Laura. 'Do you know?'

'All I know is I took a lot of notes on

it,' she said. 'Then suddenly there weren't any more to take. He said he had abandoned it. But what does it matter now? I'm sure it was destroyed. I believe that, at least.'

'You're mad, the bloody lot of you!' Grey shouted out. 'It was a failure. It went.'

Potson laughed, then got hold of the girl's arm and swung her to face him. He grabbed a handful of her yellow hair and pulled it away so that he could see both her eyes.

'The translator told you to destroy it, didn't it?' he said.

I could see he didn't know but meant to find out. Until then he seemed to have believed the story of the machine having burnt itself out.

'It couldn't,' she said. 'It didn't speak.'

'It didn't have to, did it?' he said, tense and angry. 'Didn't it fix you so that you just sat and let the signals come into your brain when the light was on? Wasn't that what happened? When that man said Light, I remembered then, of all the machines we had the only one that had to have brilliant coloured lights shining was that damned translator. Remember it? The rainbow lights? The prismatic grids? Remember them? And you looked into them while you sat there. Remember? And something happened and you weren't there, sitting in the chair but away, like up in that damned tower. Remember all that, Maggy?'

'It was just a machine! It didn't work.'

'Pretty crude thoughts it must have put into your head in place of your own,' Potson said, staring deep into her eyes as he pulled her hair and her head back. She didn't resist, seemed to be mesmerised. 'Very crude. You were always such an ingenious liar before. A twisted, tortuous liar. If you thought you were losing, you'd whip round and pile on another lie that seemed different, but made the first seem true. I remember you, Maggy, as you used to be.'

'What are you trying to do?' Grey shouted and went to go forward.

I stood in front of him, and he stopped but tried to shove me aside.

'Car!' Laura snapped out.

He stopped on the edge of fighting me to get by.

Potson went on.

'You were like that before the machine. Clever,' he said. 'But now you just say it didn't work. Where is the liar's mind gone? Why didn't it work? What brilliant burst of imagining can you bring to bear to describe the last hours of the useless machine? Didn't it explode, fling you to the ground, blow the door off, make you lose your memory? That was always the way of Maggy. Full of colour and wild exaggeration. Not now. 'It didn't work,' you say. 'It burst,' you say. They aren't your words, Maggy. They're the words of someone who doesn't understand that the human animal doesn't believe *anything*. It isn't enough to say, 'It didn't work.' The human mind needs the exaggeration, the enlargement of the picture, the colour-up. But whoever told you to say 'It didn't work' doesn't know that.'

He let her go suddenly. She fell back against the wall, silent, staring at him. He was getting into her, because he knew her so very well.

Now the machines had stopped their radiation, Potson's mind was free.

'How do I know, Maggy, that the translator did work?' he said quietly. 'Because of this. It gave you the ideas you had to keep for repetition when the light influence came again.

'This afternoon you were normal, lustful, mischievous as you always were. You kissed him, sat on his lap, teased him, as has always been your idea of amusement.

'But then, when the light influence began to approach and the weeds began to move, no more words, no more passion from you. You became a zombie, the almost speechless one, a dummy, waiting. Now and again fear burst through you like a bubble, and you shouted something, but it died again, and you were back, waiting. A toy. A toy of something you have never seen.

'Now you can tell me what really happened with the Translator.'

'It didn't work!' she cried out, but violently now, as if coming out of a trance. 'It didn't work! It didn't work!'

He grabbed her against him and held her while she tried to hit him. Then she went slack and started to cry.

'Bastard!' Grey said. He was furious, but he didn't seem to know what to do, as if some struggle took place in his volatile mind. 'We never told you!'

'What did happen to it, Grey?' I said. 'Which room was it in?'

I started towards the stairs to make him act. He did. He grabbed the newel post and put his other hand flat against the wall, barring the way.

'It has gone! It was destroyed!' he said. 'There's nothing left.'

'Let him see,' Laura said.

'No,' Grey said. 'For Christ's sake, no!'

She went close to him.

'What did happen, Car? What did happen? Let me remind you of something. You said about the man who came. The man who complained. You said he burst in there when you were trying and went out of his mind, suddenly, like that! That he just went out, blank, no memory, nothing. That he just went out and you never saw him again. Do you remember saying all that? I didn't believe you. I thought you'd made him stay, as you made this man stay, but I knew you wouldn't kill him, Car, or be cruel. I didn't know then what this man says now, that some of the ideas you got from this machine aren't yours.

'What did happen to the machine and that man?'

Suddenly Grey sat down on the stairs.

'He burnt up,' he said tonelessly. 'He went with the machine. I got out in time. He didn't. It kills.'

Like cold water dashed in my face I realized something of Grey's mad reasoning. It was that from the moment that I had met him he would not have let me go. For me, it would have been like the other caller, but the weeds had come too soon. He had stopped.

I remembered during the night he had kept saying, 'I didn't think it would be like this! I thought they would come!'

Maggy had said the same. Perhaps when the weeds had started to dance they had both begun to fear they had been cheated. She had gone dumb with unexplained fears. He had started to fight against them, but knowing it must be too late, had still kept their secret. Like Faust, he had called up the Devil from the basement and couldn't get the lid back on again.

His talk of the screaming metal, the machines, all that had been designed to interest me and keep me in that place. And it had all been true, which had given it such strength.

One could see in perspective his mad arrogance against an authority which seemed so weak beside the almost almighty he had gone into league with. Based on old grievances it had taken just that to blow it up into an insane hatred of those whose stupidity had kept him back before.

Yet, when he had found himself doublecrossed by his aliens, and his extreme views of my Ministry had proved true, he had seen the satirical side of it.

With a mind like that, there was hope for him yet, while he was still torn between his dream and the reality. Perhaps pure Irish bloodymindedness had prevented his complete takeover by the signals in the translator.

'Let me see what's left,' I said.

He shrugged then and got up. He turned and lumbered up the stairs. From somewhere above the clatter of falling bricks came again, but now nobody seemed to care. The menace outside was the greater then.

I followed Grey up to the first landing. He threw a door open and just stood there. There was no light. I shone the little torch in. There was a lot of wreckage, burnt up apparatus iced with white powder from an extinguisher. It was almost impossible to see what it had been.

'That,' he said grabbing my shoulder and pointing, 'is what's left of the man.'

There was a heap of brownish dust or ash in one corner.

'It just limed him to rubbish,' Grey said and turned away. 'There wasn't anything I could do. He said the interference came from that room, and he insisted on going in. He was a ham. He had detectors a few streets away and got a fix so accurate he could tell the floor. When he came he had a sort of radio geiger counter and it gave him the dead spot.'

'What sort of interference? I thought you said it was mostly laser?'

'It was a bastard of radio and laser, like the lot upstairs,' he said. 'What's it matter now, anyway? There's nothing inside that damned thing out there. They're just the destroyers. When they've finished, the animals will come. I didn't realize that was how they would do it. They seemed super-intelligent. But they seem just as bloody as we are.'

He leaned on the banisters and stared at nothing.

'Isn't it possible they haven't realized what their frequencies would do to our world?' I said. 'Does it have to be deliberate destruction? Couldn't it be an error?'

He didn't answer.

'From the state of the air out there,' I said, 'I reckon we shall die before the house collapses. Either way, it'll be a close thing. We shall have to get out.'

'It won't let us go from here,' he said.

'If you doubt me, look at that man in there.'

'Why do they want you, then?' I said.

'Fifth column. I don't know. Maybe they want somebody who can explain things when they get here. That's what I think.'

'By the time they get here there won't be anybody left to explain.'

'They don't understand that. I'm of the belief they're not physical as we are.'

'Then how did they build these survey towers?'

'Machines build machines. That's what we'll come to. We're well on the way now. Soon man won't do anything at all. Then he'll rot because he hasn't the brain to do anything else.'

'There isn't time for philosophical discussion. We've got to go. We can get through the weeds now. They're thinning. The less the oxygen gets the quicker they'll die.'

'So will we,' he said. 'Once out of this house we'll have to struggle and there won't be air enough to do it. But one of us is bound to be seen, and then — ' He waved his hand towards the wrecked room again. 'We've got no choice. We've had it. Console yourself. We're not the only ones.'

'Get up out of it,' I said, shaking his arm. 'There's still a chance. Out the back. The canal.'

'What about the air?'

'We'll have to risk that.'

'That thing can see through the house to the back.'

'Perhaps it could, but at the moment it isn't. We've seen it. Its on a sweep of the city at its own level. We've seen it!'

Laura called up sharply, the alarm plain in her voice.

'A man — there was a man out there!' she said.

'What man?' Grey said.

'It was a man, coming towards the house — from Mark Street — it flashed him into nothing. There's nothing there but sort — of — sort of powder.'

'On the pavement?' Grey said.

'He was coming through the weeds, very slowly — like drunk, but he had a mask.'

'Was he going towards the tower?'

'No. Coming here.'

Grey turned to me. He didn't bother to say anything. He started downstairs to the hall where the other three were.

'It's hopeless,' he said.

'But it didn't blip us,' Potson said. 'We ran out, to the tower, we came back again. It didn't blip us.'

'It's a machine,' Laura said. 'It has to work on set rules. We've got this radiation it recognizes. That's it.'

'Then how would it know if we were trying to go away?' I said.

Potson laughed.

'Okay. Then who'll be the first to try and see?'

There was a hell of a crack from somewhere and then a roar of falling bricks and stone. We turned towards the door to the machine basement. The end house had gone. We could see through the broken walls of the other houses and on to the open city sky.

I saw Laura swallow.

'It isn't much of a choice,' she said huskily. 'It's just a question of which way we go. Suffocation or just plain smothered with bricks. It might be better outside. I don't think that man felt anything.'

As the rubble settled and silence fell again, the chatter of someone calling on the radiophone in the study came as such a shock nobody seemed to know what it was.

I came to and pushed my way in past the others.

'Are you still there?' Harcourt said. 'Thank God! I thought — '

I cut in and told him what had happened to us since his last call.

'You're lucky,' he snapped. 'Things have got out of hand everywhere else. The whole countryside's crawling. The weed's coming up out of the sea, crawling up the beaches. We can't get a thing near. They're just blasting out men by the hundred when we try. Disintegration. Then they just stand still and watch the crowds choking to death. There must be some way to counteract it! There must be!'

'Have any more landed?'

'Not that we know of. They must be standing out in space to see what happens here first. Perhaps we're going to be just the bridgehead for an invasion.'

'The machine out there, it's got no pressurization or oxygen tanks. It just lets any old atmosphere get in, perhaps so it can analyse it. So it could mean these operators don't breathe — '

'You said there was nobody inside it!'

'No.' I had surprised myself. 'No, that's right. There's nothing inside, and there couldn't be anybody that wanted to breathe — '

'Hang on. More calls . . . ' He clattered away off stage and I heard voices coming at him, several at once.

I put the phone on the table and went into the hall.

'Potson!'

He was standing by the girl as she slumped in a chair, and he turned his wet, shining face to me.

'You said you sensed ghosts in this house,' I said. 'When was that?'

'A few days back,' he said. 'I said to Grey that the place stank of ghosts, but I

220

realize you could sense anything with the damned frequencies that thing was giving off. Worse than the ones up top — '

'The translator?'

'The Devil machine,' he said.

'Why did you say smell, or stink? Grey remembered that when I mentioned it myself.'

'It was just a word. Reeks, stinks. What else do you say? You can't say stuffed with or blazing with because you can feel or see, but you can smell the chill or the heat. I've been one or two places and to me it's a kind of smell.'

'And out on the car park, too?'

'All round the damn place. But then dozens of people were buried out there, blasted to bits when that rocket came down years ago. Perhaps that was at the back of my mind. I get rogue thoughts.'

Laura looked at me.

'Ring that man of yours,' she said. 'Ask if people were actually buried there on the park. There will be records.'

'Not of missing people.'

'Anyway, what are ghosts but frequency disturbances left by people when they were alive?' said Grey. 'Frequencies that don't die. You can't kill anything, in truth. Its existence must go on somehow, in some form or other — '

There was another shaking crash from the ruins of the end house. The girl jumped. Grey looked as if he had been hit. Laura got my arm. Only Potson stood still.

'Frequencies,' he said. 'That's what all this is about. Immense vibration. What makes a scream? Dissonance. Two notes making a false one. If you tune both together, the scream disappears — '

He started suddenly and ran into the study. I turned after him and saw him wrench open the music cabinet. The writhing piece of rocket metal seemed to leap out at him. He dodged back and the remnant fell to the carpet, rolling over, seeming to kick as it went. He shoved his foot on it. It struggled to get out from under, and the man's heavy body moved hard to keep the thing trapped.

Laura buried her face in my shoulder so as not to see.

Grey came beside me, slowly, like a

man slowly realizing something.

'Great Christ!' he said.

Potson bent, picked up the metal from under his foot and threw it back into the insulated cabinet. He slammed the little door so hard the case rocked.

'Hot, hot as hell,' he said, rubbing his fingers together. 'You remember when that dead man came, Grey? You remember when he came? Where was that metal then?'

'In the translator room.'

Grey wiped his face as he answered. 'I had it there. I tried to ask questions through the machine about what was making it hot and moan as it did. I asked the questions but there was no answer. Then Maggy let the man in. He started to row with me. I put the metal on the machine. Then suddenly he shouted and almost immediately the machine blew — and so did he. He had his hand on the machine . . . '

He wiped his face again.

'I got the extinguisher on the landing. It was too late. It stopped a fire. Nothing else. The metal was screaming then. I brought it downstairs and put it back. I had to keep it, you see . . . It was an order — '

'If that rocket came down out there, went into the ground and then blew out and upwards, there are plenty more bits of that metal down under the park,' Potson said, his face running sweat. 'Our theory's wrong. It wasn't you who brought these things. They made you bring them! That's what it was, Grey. They made you!'

The big man stood there, staring through Potson.

'I begin to see — ' he said, then stopped as if he had lost his thoughts.

'When did you first stumble on this rig up that gave you these wayout frequencies?' Potson said. 'Try and think!'

'I remember now,' Grey said. 'You needn't worry. I remember. I found that bit of tin out there on the park. When I found where it came from it started me thinking along lines of interplanetary signalling. I kept that piece as a mascot. I thought if I got a system which got ahead of the clumsy ones everybody else was using I'd get my own back for the way the sods had treated me.'

He started to laugh, then stopped abruptly.

'And sometime after that the ideas of the circuits just came,' Potson said.

'They seemed natural developments.'

'In spite of the fact that nobody else on this earth had got the same ideas?' Potson challenged. 'You must be a born big head, Grey! You alone, working alone — how did it seem possible for you to beat the big battalions with all their scientific resources? How could you think it was all coming from your brain?'

Grey just nodded. The madness had gone out of him.

'Okay,' Potson said. 'Euclidize. The rocket was contaminated with alien sperm. It came here, burst and the sperm was incubated. In time it began to create itself, recreate, grow. People began to notice something was wrong and went.

'The minute creatures — if you can call them that — infesting the metal of the forgotten rocket, were alive and starting to work. They discover Grey and his radio nearby. They find an ordinary gifted ham who had bought the standing houses because of the desolation. Because of the rocket.

'What are these things? Animation germs. Ideas, we would say. Influences. They start Grey working. They get his hook-up complete so at last they — not him, but *they* — can communicate with their own lot. That's why these towers came Grey. That's why the invasion. To join with the lost ones of years ago.

'These towers didn't come out to invade us. They couldn't have covered the distance from that star in the time. They must have a permanent space patrol of these things somewhere, patrols that go in when something like this happens.

'The rocket must have picked the contamination from a patrol. A near one, because rockets don't go that far out into space. At the time, nothing was noticed. But the germs grew up and the signal went out — not to Sirius — as you imagined, but to a patrol station, and in came the avengers.

'We saw them spectrum analysing, man

analysing. Why? What do they want to find? Copper? Salt? No. They want to find exactly where their own are. They know it's in this country and the centre is here outside this room, but they mean to make sure there is no splash to other places where the V2s fell. That's what the survey's for. It's a search. What else can all this be?'

'The weeds,' Laura said. 'What about the weeds?'

'The frequencies have been speeding things up,' Potson said. 'I don't go back on that. I agree with the pundits. It's a side effect, not the main development. Though it looks like being a main development if it goes on any longer.'

'You may be right, Jack,' Maggy said, getting up very slowly. 'You may be dead right. You're a mathematician, so you like to be right. But how in hell does this help us now?'

★   ★   ★

More bricks and stuff crashed down, closer now. We heard it clanging down on

227

the machines in the basement.

'First thing,' I said, picking up the phone again, 'you tell Harcourt what your initial steps were. It may be possible for the big stations to hook one up like yours.'

'What then?' Grey said.

'Just do that first,' I said. Harcourt answered. I gave him Grey after telling him to keep his tapes rolling on the talk.

Grey spoke very shortly, as if he didn't want to speak at all. He put it all so clearly that even I almost understood what he was getting at. He was sweating hard. The air was getting thin. Outside the window the weeds were dying fast.

Some questions were asked — obviously not by Harcourt but some experts he had there. Grey barked the answers, some of them in figures.

Outside the window the metal sentinel kept watch with its spinning bowl never varying its speed.

Grey finished. There was a long shiffing from the falling buildings at the end, a clatter here and there, then a groan and stillness again for a while.

'That's why that door opened,' Maggy said, wonderingly. 'We've not got radiation. We've got the bloody things in us! That's why the door opened! They're in us, too!'

'Ghosts,' said Potson, hoarsely. 'Just think of them like that and not as physical things. Obviously they're not physical. Not even germs. Ghosts, as the science man said.'

He looked at me and flashed a grin, then sat down at the table and looked at Grey.

'We've got to do something,' he said.

'What?' Grey said.

'You've got more in your mind of these things than we have,' Potson said. 'What would placate them, persuade them or just plain jam them up?'

'I don't know,' Grey said.

Laura let go of my arm at last.

'We've been wrong all the time,' she said. 'This house still stands and we're still here, not because of anything we've got or done, but because we're contaminated and because that awful wriggling thing is in here!'

'What does it matter?' Maggy said. 'The house is falling on us. If we try and go we'll die for breath or get turned into soot out there. So what does any of it matter? All this talk is just whistling in the dark!'

'Why give up?' Laura said.

'You have!' Maggy said.

'I only give up for a few seconds. Then I start again,' Laura said. 'If you weren't so damned ME all the time it would be easier.'

'Why should you criticize?' Maggy said. 'If you hadn't been so damn ME you would have married him and I might not have been an illegitimate frustration.'

'I did marry him,' Laura said. 'It was a long way back. It didn't work. So we decided not to.'

'You decided not to?' Maggy said. She wasn't incredulous, just furious. 'Not to what? To leave me a ripe bastard in need of a mother's love?'

'I had a career,' Laura said. 'At that time I had to pretend to be single. We'd separated. So we went on with our separate works. Didn't Leila look after you well? My poor sister always wanted a child.'

I realized at this stage that the oxygen lack was in. The two women were just fighting each other, talking rubbish. The thin air was coming in. Weakness that led to death.

The phone began to chatter. I picked it up.

'We can hitch this up, Richard,' Harcourt said. 'But what do we do with it?'

'Where are you doing it?' I said.

'Everywhere we have enough equipment in or near the landing points.'

'Why didn't you say you were married?' Maggy said.

'He wouldn't have got his money, then,' Laura said.

'Let's get out of here,' Potson said. 'No matter what way. We've told everybody. If we blow up, they'll know what to do now we've told them.'

'Just sit down. Let it come,' Maggy said. 'You won't stop it, because this is It. Gory finish. What can you do? Or the man at the Ministry with all his horses and men? None of you can do anything, for why? Because They know what you're doing while you're doing it. How can you keep it secret? They're right in you, and me and father and mother — everybody!'

'The dear girl's essentially bloody correct,' Grey said, and practically collapsed into a chair at the table. 'There's nothing to do.'

The tower was still, its bowl translucent against the sky, the silent killer.

'Perhaps they don't understand we need oxygen,' Laura said. 'Perhaps they don't know what kills us.'

'You are a generous woman,' Grey said. 'Haven't they been here all these years, getting to know what kills us? What have they been doing, if they don't know these elemental facts by now? Are they stupid? Didn't they do what they wanted with us? If they did that, don't they understand what makes us tick?'

Potson was sitting now, head bent, watching his sweat dripping from his face to his breasts and running down his belly.

'It isn't essential to give in,' he said to the sweat drops. 'One does not have to fail all the time. Not all the time.'

He was talking to himself, repeating it over and over, a man persuading himself he is all right when he isn't.

In the weakness of my body and in irritation because I knew I was losing control of it, I let a burst of fury suck even more energy out of me. I heard the women talking aimlessly, trying to argue with each other, making no sense.

'We must hurry,' Potson told his running sweat. 'There's no time. But the solution is always there. Always there. Always there. It remains but to work it out.'

'Shut up, you porpoise!' I shouted.

'I knew this would happen,' Grey said.

He went to lift his mug to his lips but half way there was a struggle for the necessary strength and he let it back to the table again.

The vision of all these things was clear then, and is now. The vision, even the understanding, but the strength to do anything about it had gone.

As we sat there, just propped up round the room, I was where I could see through the door, across the hall and to the open end of the houses where the oxygen we had had was oozing out.

'If you went and started up your radar again,' I said, 'you might contact them. You might say something they would understand.'

'If we said we were dying — ' said Potson, almost comfortably.

'What would they care?' said Maggy. 'Things like that don't feel anything or care anything — '

Harcourt was cricketting on the phone. I sat and looked at it.

'Answer the man,' Potson said, without looking up.

'It isn't worth it,' I said.

There was another shattering avalanche from the collapsing houses and the scene of the open sky beyond the hall changed. Its frame became a different shape.

'Why doesn't it fall in here?' Maggy said.

'Start up the radar,' Potson said. 'Get some pretty blips.'

'I thought I saw it taking off again,' Laura said.

She was looking through the window, leaning her chin on her hands, elbows on the table.

'You didn't do anything,' Maggy said. 'You never do anything. Why didn't you get married? You stupid cow. Why didn't you ever think of me? What's your career, anyhow? You'll be dead in a minute. Then it won't matter. It's all cosines. He always says cosines. Contraceptives and cosines. It all figures, but it's in there all the time. Inside you. Thousands of the bloody things. Crawling about inside you. Contaminated bugs — '

Harcourt clattered again. I leant my face sideways on the table.

'We're trying to contact — Can you hear me?' he said.

'We're all dying,' I said.

'Not soon enough,' Maggy said. 'It's a dead bore when you can't do anything and it's all because they didn't play fair with me — '

'We're trying to get in over the back of you,' Harcourt said. 'But two hundred feet over your sixty gives it too steep an angle without hitting the house. They blasted out sixty men so far. Didn't you hear anything?'

I just lay there looking at the phone. It was very peaceful. Nobody ever thought of a better way, except that the breathing was very hard.

I shoved against the table edge to get myself up again.

'We can't get out the back either,' I said. 'That ray goes over — '

'Eat something,' Laura said. 'Strength.'

'Make an effort,' Potson said, hoisting himself upright in the chair. 'Think. Reason. A way in. Must be a way out. Fight back.'

'Fight back,' Grey repeated. 'There's some big bloody fools round here. I'm sorry I ever came to England. A lot of bigots in triplicate — '

'The thing they want's in the cupboard,' Laura said, making an effort. 'Throw it out at them. Throw their ball back. They might go.'

'If we do that, they'll blast the place,' said Grey, almost bored.

'Why bother?' Maggy said. 'It'll fall anyhow.'

'They're hard men, these things,' Potson said. 'If anything gets in the way — blam! No feeling. Just hard. But they want their own. Praps they're dying out there on Sirius. Praps the few remaining are valuable. So they have to rescue as many as they can. Thirty years to incubate, or whatever you say. Thirty years. You can't afford to lose any if they're thinning out. Otherwise why have such a big patrol to try and get the little ones back — '

Potson heaved himself out of the chair. It creaked under him.

'The Q.E.D. has come,' he said. 'Or if it hasn't, by the time we know it won't matter.'

He bent and pulled the thick tablecloth off, scattering books and papers everywhere.

'Get that bloody screaming thing out of there, Grey!' he shouted.

His idea gave him new strength. It did us too. Fat and ungainly, yet he seemed to have a kind of inspiration radiating from him. In dying despair, perhaps it did not need much to animate us with the ghost of a straw.

'Get it out!'

Potson almost fell over but hit the table instead. The castors screamed on the floor. The edge hit Grey and tipped his chair over backwards. He got up by climbing over the overturned legs.

I got to my feet by holding the table and fishing for the phone which Potson had sent to dangle on its own wire.

'Frequency, frequency,' said Potson. 'That's their existence and ours. But we've got many because we're solid. They've got few, perhaps one. Cart it upstairs, Grey. Cart the survivors of Sirius up those bloody stairs and get your radar set so it beams right on that bit of tin instead of up into the sky. Bore it with frequency. Alter the tune till it stops screaming at you. Alter it till the living things in there are suddenly nullified by the harmonic. Paralyse them. Show these patrolmen that you can kill their patrons. Show them they're vulnerable. You know what then? They'll go. If they know they can be beat, they'll go, Grey! They'll go!'

We got the writhing metal out of the

cabinet and into the tablecloth. Harcourt was barking on the phone, but he had heard what Potson said. It was on the Ministry tapes. All of it was on the tapes.

'You've got the frequency, Grey, up there,' Potson chanted as we staggered and reeled in the long journey up the stairs. 'You've got the bomb. It just wants fusing. They taught you the frequency. Show them the equal and opposite reaction. Show them!'

He almost sang as we went slowly up. The falling of more of the buildings was an accompaniment that somehow we did not care about any more.

We didn't even think what would happen when the machines below started thumping about again.

The women followed, pulling themselves up on the handrail. I remember calling back to them, looking back to them. It was no time to separate.

When we got to the top Potson was on his hands and knees walking doglike, dragging the cloth and the wriggling thing inside it like a burglar with his loot.

We got into the radar room. Grey

recovered a little at the nearness of his machinery.

'Get it in the bowl, the forward bowl,' he said, falling against the wall screen. 'Get it in the bowl!'

It seemed all four of us fought to get the cloth up and tip the wriggling obscenity into the first radar bowl. The small aerial was stationary then. Grey started switching things over in the corner. Lights came on in the bowls, and the scanners started to rotate, then stopped abruptly.

'Now put it in front of the saucer,' Grey panted. 'In front of the saucer.'

The metal was twisting and rolling and giving off that siren-like screaming.

The juice came on. We felt the machines in the basement start up, thumping and shaking the breaking building.

'It won't work!' Maggy cried out. 'It's no good!'

'I'm increasing!' Grey said.

He leaned against the wall operating the controls on his panel.

Suddenly everything locked solid in

silence. The metal became rigid, the screaming stopped, the thunder of the machines below all ceased.

I think we all ceased, too.

Part of the wall broke away by Grey, slowly, almost thoughtfully. Part of the night sky showed there as the soft rattle of the bricks down the outer walls fell away into silence.

'Has it — ?' Laura said that.

'It's stopped,' Potson said. 'It's bloody well stopped!'

But he was pointing to the top of the blue metal tower through the rent in the wall. The bowl had stopped spinning. The search was over for the patrol. The Achilles heel had been uncovered.

We watched the tower begin to shrink back into itself, quickly, silently.

'Go down,' I said. 'Get Harcourt. Get that chopper back. Tell it to bring oxygen.'

The disc went within thirty seconds of the bowl stopping. It went with a screaming as it had come, creating a gas skin round itself as it went upward into the hazy sky.

By the time the chopper came over, there was only half the centre house left. We were in a corner of the radar room, crowding over the electric motors, trying to get what little ozone they had to give off in that thin, burning air.

When Potson was winched up into the helicopter he, like the rest of us, had an oxygen mask clapped over his face. He gulped a lot and as we started to rise, he pulled it aside.

'It's ideas that count,' he said. 'Screaming. I never could stand high pitched voices. Then I remembered the singer who shattered a wineglass by getting the right note that shook it to death. Everything is very simple when one takes it Euclid's way.'

I looked down as we swung away over the remains of Nelson Street. The central house was toppling then, but not falling over, just sort of rippling, gently cascading its upper slates and bricks downwards, like someone emptying a bucket of sand.

THE MAYHEM MADCHEN
THE DEATH IMPORTER
THE THUG EXECUTIVE
A WREATH OF BONES
THE CASE OF THE FEAR MAKERS
A FALL-OUT OF THIEVES
THE FARM VILLAINS
FATE OF THE LYING JADE

We do hope that you have enjoyed reading this large print book.

Did you know that all of our titles are available for purchase?

We publish a wide range of high quality large print books including:
Romances, Mysteries, Classics
General Fiction
Non Fiction and Westerns

Special interest titles available in large print are:
The Little Oxford Dictionary
Music Book, Song Book
Hymn Book, Service Book

Also available from us courtesy of Oxford University Press:
Young Readers' Dictionary
(large print edition)
Young Readers' Thesaurus
(large print edition)

For further information or a free brochure, please contact us at:
Ulverscroft Large Print Books Ltd.,
The Green, Bradgate Road, Anstey,
Leicester, LE7 7FU, England.
Tel: (00 44) 0116 236 4325
Fax: (00 44) 0116 234 0205

THE SILVERED CAGE

John Russell Fearn

For an illusionist to make a woman vanish from a cage is merely stock-in-trade, because the woman must go somewhere. But when the woman concerned really does disappear, in full view of an audience, it is the commencement of a baffling puzzle for Scotland Yard. Bogged down in the mists of stage magic, they enlist the aid of the indomitable Dr Carruthers, a specialist in scientific jig-saws, and it is he who finally solves what happened to the woman and explains away the brilliant ingenuity of the vanishing act.

PICK UP THE PIECES

J. F. Straker

Andrew White, the proprietor of a country garage, sees four of his mechanics run over a woman while they are on an unauthorized ride in a customer's car. Thinking there had been no witnesses, they fail to report the accident. White then blackmails the men. Soon desperate, they plan to steal White's savings, drawing lots to decide who shall break in, and agreeing that the thief shall remain anonymous. The next morning, White is found murdered, his savings stolen. But someone knows their secret and plans to profit by it . . .

END OF THE LINE

George Douglas

There had to be a good reason why old Miss Harvill, of the Dower House, Fenton, was killed. The trouble was there were too many suspects. Detective Inspector Lynn, the officer in charge of the case, finds complications arising when some of the girls from Fenton Manor School seem to be implicated in odd incidents in the vicinity of the Dower House. When one of the girls goes missing, a clever piece of observation, aided by specialised knowledge, leads a constable to what proves to be her grave . . .

THE HARASSED HERO

Ernest Dudley

Murray Selwyn, six-foot-two and athletic, was so convinced he had not long to live that when he came across a hold-up, a murder and masses of forged fivers, he was too worried about catching a chill to give them much attention. But when he met his pretty nurse, Murray began to forget his ailments, and by the end of a breath-taking chase after some very plausible crooks, the hypochondriac had become a hero.